TOO PRETTY TO DIE

EVA RAE THOMAS MYSTERY - BOOK 13

WILLOW ROSE

Join Willow Rose's VIP Newsletter to get exclusive updates about New Releases, Giveaways, and FREE ebooks.

Just scan this QR code with your phone and click on the link:

SCAN ME

Tired of too many emails? Text the word: "willowrose" to 31996 to sign up to Willow's VIP text List to get a text alert with news about New Releases, Giveaways, Bargains and Free books from Willow.

FOLLOW WILLOW ROSE ON BOOKBUB:

Connect with Willow online:
https://www.facebook.com/willowredrose/
https://twitter.com/madamwillowrose
http://www.goodreads.com/author/show
https://www.willow-rose.net
madamewillowrose@gmail.com

Books by the Author

HARRY HUNTER MYSTERY SERIES

- ALL THE GOOD GIRLS
- RUN GIRL RUN
- NO OTHER WAY
- NEVER WALK ALONE

MARY MILLS MYSTERY SERIES

- WHAT HURTS THE MOST
- YOU CAN RUN
- YOU CAN'T HIDE
- CAREFUL LITTLE EYES

EVA RAE THOMAS MYSTERY SERIES

- SO WE LIE
- DON'T LIE TO ME
- WHAT YOU DID
- NEVER EVER
- SAY YOU LOVE ME
- LET ME GO
- IT'S NOT OVER
- NOT DEAD YET
- TO DIE FOR
- SUCH A GOOD GIRL
- LITTLE DID SHE KNOW
- YOU BETTER RUN
- SAY IT ISN'T SO

- TOO PRETTY TO DIE

EMMA FROST SERIES

- ITSY BITSY SPIDER
- MISS DOLLY HAD A DOLLY
- RUN, RUN AS FAST AS YOU CAN
- CROSS YOUR HEART AND HOPE TO DIE
- PEEK-A-BOO I SEE YOU
- TWEEDLEDUM AND TWEEDLEDEE
- EASY AS ONE, TWO, THREE
- THERE'S NO PLACE LIKE HOME
- SLENDERMAN
- WHERE THE WILD ROSES GROW
- WALTZING MATHILDA
- DRIP DROP DEAD
- BLACK FROST

JACK RYDER SERIES

- HIT THE ROAD JACK
- SLIP OUT THE BACK JACK
- THE HOUSE THAT JACK BUILT
- BLACK JACK
- GIRL NEXT DOOR
- HER FINAL WORD
- DON'T TELL

REBEKKA FRANCK SERIES

- ONE, TWO...HE IS COMING FOR YOU
- THREE, FOUR...BETTER LOCK YOUR DOOR
- FIVE, SIX...GRAB YOUR CRUCIFIX
- SEVEN, EIGHT...GONNA STAY UP LATE

- Nine, Ten...Never Sleep Again
- Eleven, Twelve...Dig and Delve
- Thirteen, Fourteen...Little Boy Unseen
- Better Not Cry
- Ten Little Girls
- It Ends Here

MYSTERY/THRILLER/HORROR NOVELS

- Sorry Can't Save You
- In One Fell Swoop
- Umbrella Man
- Blackbird Fly
- To Hell in a Handbasket
- Edwina

HORROR SHORT-STORIES

- Mommy Dearest
- The Bird
- Better watch out
- Eenie, Meenie
- Rock-a-Bye Baby
- Nibble, Nibble, Crunch
- Humpty Dumpty
- Chain Letter

PARANORMAL SUSPENSE/ROMANCE NOVELS

- In Cold Blood
- The Surge
- Girl Divided

THE VAMPIRES OF SHADOW HILLS SERIES

- Flesh and Blood
- Blood and Fire
- Fire and Beauty
- Beauty and Beasts
- Beasts and Magic
- Magic and Witchcraft
- Witchcraft and War
- War and Order
- Order and Chaos
- Chaos and Courage

THE AFTERLIFE SERIES

- Beyond
- Serenity
- Endurance
- Courageous

THE WOLFBOY CHRONICLES

- A Gypsy Song
- I am WOLF

DAUGHTERS OF THE JAGUAR

- Savage
- Broken

The Blind cannot see, the proud will not.

-Russian Proverb

Prologue

Miami, FL

Chapter 1

WHAT WAS it about taking a trip that made mature and otherwise very rational women go crazy and act like teenagers on prom night? It's not like they intended to let it get this far. They didn't come to Miami to party. They didn't mean for these things to happen or to become this drunk. After all, they were just four women—mothers and housewives—from Russell Springs, Kentucky, going away for a weekend of self-care.

They were doing something good for themselves for once.

As soon as they stepped off the plane and felt the warm Miami breeze on their faces, they knew deep down that this trip would be different. They were tired of being confined to their daily routines and always putting their families first. They wanted to let loose, have fun, and feel alive again.

They all had children the same age, and that's how they met—at their mom's group fifteen years ago. They quickly became friends for life. Best friends for life. Each other's *ride or die*, they would say when clinking their wine glasses. It was a cliché, but from the outside, the four of them seemed to have it all: money, looks, families, and each other.

At first, they tried to stick to their plan of relaxation and rejuvenation. They went to the spa, got massages, and lounged by the pool. But as the sun began to set, they found themselves drawn to the nightclubs and bars that lined the streets of South Beach.

It started with a few drinks, just to loosen up and have some fun. But soon enough, they were dancing on tables and flirting with strangers. They knew it was reckless and dangerous but couldn't help themselves. It was like they were teenagers again, with no responsibilities or consequences to worry about.

Kristen Thomasson, a forty-year-old middle school English teacher, was looking at her three friends at the club that night in Miami while filming them with her phone. She felt happy inside—happy to be with her best friends. Heck, she was away from her two children of seven and fifteen years, who took up all her energy and strength these days.

She had good reason to feel joy.

Yes, there was a sadness inside her that kept coming back whenever she tried to push it away and tell herself not to worry—that this was the weekend of fun. It still crept back into her mind and made her tear up.

"Come on, dance with us," Janice said, waving at her. Janice was a mental health counselor and the mother of the group, always concerned with everyone's well-being and constantly aware of everyone's mood. There was no hiding you had a bad day from her. She could tell from the moment she laid eyes on you.

"What's up?" was her favorite phrase, followed by a slightly tilted head. Her red shoulder-length hair would brush on her shoulders, and her lips pout slightly. She had an expression that made you realize you had to give her something, or she wouldn't let it go.

"I'll be right there," Kristen said and waved back. "Gonna get some more drinks." She yelled the words, but Janice signaled that she couldn't hear her because of the loud music in the club.

Kristen signaled back by pretending to be drinking from an imaginary glass, and Janice understood, then nodded and gave her a thumbs up. She didn't have to tell her what she wanted. Kristen knew her drink of choice.

"Cosmopolitan with extra cranberry juice and Grey Goose Vodka."

She yelled the words, and the twenty-year-old bartender nodded.

"And a lemon drop martini, one glass of prosecco, and an espresso martini."

"You got it," the bartender said, preparing the drinks.

Kristen watched him pour the Cosmo into the glass, then glanced at her friends on the dance floor, giving it all they had, despite being, by far, the oldest ones there. Pat was twerking, and that made her laugh. Pat could pull it off, though. She still managed to work as a model at the age of thirty-eight and had gotten her body right back after giving birth, much to the envy of the others. You couldn't even tell she had ever been pregnant on the skin of her stomach.

It wasn't fair.

She didn't make her living by being a model alone, though, as the jobs were long in between since she had reached a more mature age. For extra income, Pat worked as a real estate agent for million-dollar houses, where looking good wasn't exactly an obstacle to success.

She was the beauty of the group and the one who attracted everyone's attention whenever they went places, something especially Marley envied or maybe admired. Marley was a stay-at-home mom by choice. She wanted to focus on the upbringing and education of her only daughter, and family was everything to her. She never understood why Pat had left her husband after seven years of a miserable marriage. She had no respect for the fact that she could do such a thing and did not understand her decision to ruin a perfect family.

"She didn't even try to fight for them," was her argument. But Marley would never say so to Pat's face, only to the others when Pat wasn't there. Pat knew how she felt, though, and decided to ignore it.

She loved her friend group way too much to pick a fight and destroy what they had. Heck, they all did.

They needed each other too much to risk it.

"Cheers!"

Kristen yelled the word out as her friends approached the bar and grabbed their drinks. They all clinked their glasses, then looked at one another while sipping their drinks. As the alcohol hit their lips, Kristen felt a rush of excitement that coursed through her veins. She had been waiting for this night for weeks—a night out with her closest friends, away from the stress of work and daily life.

The bar was packed, and the music was loud, but Kristen didn't mind. She loved the crowd's energy, the way everyone seemed lost in their own world. It was a vibrant atmosphere, and Kristen felt nothing could bring her down.

AS THE NIGHT WENT ON, their group moved from the bar back to the dance floor. Kristen felt the beat of the music pulsing through her body as she let herself go, moving to the rhythm. Her friends were right beside her, and for a moment, she felt like nothing else in the world mattered.

As they danced, a man caught Kristen's eye. He was tall, with dark hair and piercing blue eyes. Kristen felt a tingle run down her spine but ignored it. Before she knew it, the man had sauntered over to her and offered to buy her and her friends a drink.

"To a night we will always remember," Marley said, lifting her shot glass to meet the others.

"Or to one we will *not* remember," Pat corrected her, laughing.

"Or to one we won't *want* to remember," Janice said with a wink.

Chapter 2

THE FIRST THING she noticed was the heat. There was this burning sensation coming from outside of her body. Pat was deep in sleep, or maybe even passed out, when she opened her eyes and suddenly realized what was happening.

Fire!

Panicking, she sat up and tried to find her bearings. The heat was unbearable, and she could barely breathe. She realized that she was out at sea, on the deck of a boat—a yacht that had flames coming up from the cabins below, licking at the sky.

Where am I?

She rose to her feet, holding onto the railing as the world spun while fear rushed through her veins. She couldn't see the others anywhere and didn't remember whose boat they were on.

How did I get here? Where is my phone?

She searched for it but didn't find it. She then looked at the ocean surrounding her and realized she couldn't see any land anywhere—only the blue and green waters as far as the eye could see—not even another boat in sight.

The yacht groaned and sighed. A window below deck popped, and Pat jumped in fear. She felt so strange—like the world around her was wobbly, and her hands and feet were detached. Her head spun massively, and she could have sworn she was in a dream, yet somehow, she knew it was real. This was very real. The fire was very real indeed.

The others? Where are the others?

"Kristen? Janice? Marley?"

Pat screamed their names in deep confusion. She saw fish in the water below her as she looked down. She knew there were big fish in these waters, and definitely also sharks.

Holding onto the railing, she slid around the deck, trying to reach the stern to see if there was a dingy or anything she could use to escape.

If there had been one, it was gone now.

Panic erupted in her as the boat creaked and moaned. The fire was spreading fast now and eating from the deck.

"Janice? Marley? Kristen?"

She screamed at the top of her lungs, but no one answered. And the yacht was beginning to sink.

Think fast, Pat. Think!

She stared at the ocean below, then searched for life jackets under the seats in the back and found one. She put it on, heart hammering in her chest, then looked out at the ocean before her, fear pounding inside her.

She had always been terrified of sharks. Beyond terrified.

"Okay, here we go," she said and was about to jump when she saw movement coming up behind her and turned her head with a gasp.

If it was the scuba mask itself or the loud breathing coming from behind it that scared her half to death, she didn't know.

As this person grabbed her throat and stabbed her in the abdomen with the fishing knife, it dawned on her that the real tragedy wasn't her dying.

It was the fact that no one knew where she was, and her body would never be found.

Part I
MIAMI, FLORIDA.

Three years later

Chapter 1

"SO, how does it feel to be here? In the same place your mom was last seen three years ago?"

Tara looked into the camera behind the woman across from her. Her eyes were big and wide. Her lip quivered slightly as she spoke.

"I... have to say, it's harder than I thought it would be."

"Please, look at me when you answer and not into the camera," the journalist said. Her name was Barbara Bowen, and she worked for a true crime show called *What Really Happened*. She looked an awful lot like her name sister Barbara Walters, with the same perfectly coiffed bob haircut and a blue power suit. It probably wasn't a coincidence, Tara thought to herself. Tara dreamt of becoming a journalist one day, and at the age of eighteen, she hadn't seen much of Barbara Walters' work, but she had read a lot about her and felt inspired to become like her one day.

Apparently, she wasn't the only one.

"I'm sorry," she said. "I have never... done anything like this before."

"I know," Barbara said with a smile. "We'll just do it again. Don't worry about it."

Tara rubbed her fingers together. They felt clammy, not just because she was so nervous but also because of the Miami heat. It was Tara's first time in Florida, and she had to admit it was hot, even though it was November. She kind of liked it and understood why her mother had chosen to go there when she was going away with her friends three years ago.

Exactly to the date.

Tara took a deep breath, trying to steady herself. It was hard to be here, but it was also something she had to do. Her mother had disappeared without a trace, leaving Tara and her dad devastated and heartbroken. They had searched for her everywhere, but no one had seen or heard from her since she left for that trip. Tara had grown up so much since then, but the pain of her mother's disappearance never left her.

Looking up, she met Barbara's eyes, feeling a sense of comfort and understanding there. The woman was a professional but also kind, which meant a lot to Tara.

"You ready?" Barbara said.

Tara swallowed and nodded. She wondered about her long brown hair and if it still looked good. She had straightened it at the hotel this morning but risked getting curls and messing up the entire thing with the heat and humidity. She looked awful with curly hair.

"Okay, let's try again," Tara said, her voice a little stronger this time.

Barbara nodded, adjusting the microphone clipped to Tara's shirt.

"Okay, let's roll."

Barbara signaled the cameraman, Billy, standing behind her, and the red light turned on again. Tara felt more nervous because she had messed up the first time.

"Tara. Your mom disappeared here in Miami, along with her three friends. Today, it's been exactly three years since she was seen last. How does it feel to be here?"

Tara cleared her throat. She felt the blood leave her face and blinked a few times, hoping the dizziness would disappear. Barbara smiled and nodded, urging her to start talking.

"It… I guess it's a lot harder than I thought it would be."

"And why is that?"

Tara took a deep breath. Her heart was hammering in her chest, yet she felt herself growing pale. The walls in the hotel lobby were closing in, or so it felt. Was she going to pass out?

You can't faint. Not now.

"Are you okay?" Barbara asked.

Tara closed her eyes briefly and then nodded. "Yes, yes, I just need a moment."

"Take your time."

Tara cleared her throat again. She opened her eyes and looked at Barbara. "I'm sorry, it's just really… I haven't seen my mom since I was fifteen years old, and I thought it would be easy to come here, but it is really hard. To know that she was here, and this is one of the places she was, and where some man at the front desk saw her according to the police report, it's just…."

"Overwhelming," Barbara said with a sympathetic smile.

Tara nodded. "Yes. It's a lot."

"So, now that you have come here, what do you expect to find?"

She shook her head. "I don't really know. I mean, I want to find out what happened to her, but so far, they haven't been able to figure it out, and it's been three years, so…."

"You don't have much confidence in the police and trust that they will find out?"

She shook her head with a deep exhale. "Not really."

"But I take it you would like to have some sort of closure, right?"

She nodded. "Yes. That's why we're here—all four of us. We've had this big gap inside us for all these years, and we just need to know something. Anything. It's hard to move on, you know? When you have no answers."

"Let's hope we can get some on this trip then."

Tara smiled. "That would be nice. That would be really nice."

Barbara nodded, then signaled for the cameraman Billy to stop. She smiled at Tara, who felt nervous still.

"Thank you. That's enough for now," Barbara said.

"Was I okay?" Tara asked. "Did I do well enough?"

Barbara placed both hands on her shoulders. "You were amazing, my dear. We will continue later and go into more detail."

"Okay, thank you," Tara said and hurried away. On the way to the elevator of the hotel, she met Scott. He smiled awkwardly at her as they passed one another, and he approached Barbara, then sat down in the chair across from her.

"Scott, tell me about your mother," she heard Barbara say as she entered the elevator. The doors closed, and she could finally breathe again. She and Scott had been childhood friends, but ever since their mothers disappeared, they hadn't seen each other much, other than the casual passing of each other in the hallways at the high school or the mall. But as the years passed, they hadn't even said hello to one another anymore. That went for Kim and Mike as well. Back when they were children, their mothers had been best friends, so they had many playdates, the four of them, throughout their entire childhood. But once their mothers disappeared, that stopped, and now they had been brought together again by this TV show that wanted to dig deeper into what really happened to them. Tara was excited, even though she was initially reluctant because she was a little scared of what they might discover. But Scott and Mike hadn't wanted to go, yet Tara and Kim had persuaded them to say yes.

"If we're ever going to find out what happened three years ago, this is it," Kim had argued when they all met up at their old playground in their hometown of Russell Springs, Kentucky. "We need to say yes to this or forever give up knowing why our mothers never came home."

Chapter 2

"ARE YOU KIDDING ME WITH THIS?"

The guy in the blue polo shirt shook his head. He must have been around twenty years younger than me. He was holding an iPad in his hand, where he had just shown me the quotes of what it would cost them to fix my electricity. My house was old, from the sixties, and after two hurricanes hitting Cocoa Beach this year, I had a lot of damage. My windows desperately needed to be changed as water had come in during the storms. The ceiling had water damage, and so did the floors. Honestly, it felt like the house was falling apart with me still in it.

"That's the initial quote," he said. "It could be more expensive if it turns out that the wiring is more complicated underground. We need to get in first to see how it is put together. But it's completely rusted away, and it's only a matter of time before it falls apart, and then you won't have any power."

"But seventeen thousand dollars? You can't be serious?" I asked, feeling how the air in my lungs grew tight. I didn't have that kind of money. "I'm a single mom with four children. How do you expect me to pay that?"

He gave me a look, then shrugged. "It's definitely something you will need to think about."

"You think?"

"But I wouldn't wait too long," he said. "Or you risk it getting more expensive."

I smiled sarcastically. "I figured you'd say something like that."

"Of course, it's up to you," he said, throwing out his long, thin arms.

I pinched the bridge of my nose and sighed. "I will definitely need to think this over. But thank you for coming out."

He walked to the door. "I'm sorry to be the bearer of such bad news."

I smiled politely, struggling to hide that I wanted to scream. "It's not your fault."

He left, and I closed the door, slamming it a little too hard after him. Then I walked to the kitchen and sank into my chair, phone in hand, looking at the quote the guy had just sent me in an email.

Where the heck was I supposed to find seventeen thousand dollars? I still hadn't gotten the quote on the two new windows either, but that was probably up there as well.

How was I supposed to afford this?

How could I afford not to?

The next storm that came along would completely destroy whatever was left. I had filed a claim with the insurance company, but they hid behind the fact that my house was already old and called the damages wear and tear.

Wear and tear, yes, but worn and torn by a freaking hurricane.

I rubbed my forehead and put down the phone. I walked to the coffee pot and poured myself a cup. I sipped it, then looked at the pack of Oreos my kids had left on the table. I wanted desperately to take one, but I had lost ten pounds since I started to cut back on junk food, and I didn't want to regain it all.

I spotted Matt pulling up into my driveway. He took Angel out from the back seat and walked up toward the house. I checked myself in the mirror, then sighed. It didn't really matter what I did these days; I still looked exhausted. Meanwhile, Matt looked like a dream, as always. I don't know how he did it.

Maybe it was just because I was dealing with four children. Having both teenagers and a toddler in the house wasn't exactly a walk in the park.

"Hey, I just saw the electrician pull out of your driveway?" Matt said.

Angel smiled when she saw me and reached for me. He handed her to me, and I hugged her tight. I hated when she was at his house because I missed her so much. But it was a welcome break for me now and then. And I needed that.

"Yeah, I just got a quote to fix things around the house. It's all rusting away, apparently. Because we live so close to the ocean, the salt is eating at everything."

He gave me a look. "That sounds expensive. And you said that you're getting new windows too?"

"Yeah, well," I sighed. "Maybe I'll have to do just one of those two—probably the electricity since it could get dangerous."

"You can't. Those windows won't last through another hurricane."

I closed my eyes briefly. "Thanks for reminding me. Did everything go well with Angel?"

"Yeah, she was really good. We went to the playground for about an hour or so. She should be ready for her nap... say, are you having money trouble?"

I stared at him, biting my lip. There was no way I would ever tell him the truth. I shook my head.

"No, no. It's fine. Just a lot of trouble, you know?"

"Well, you let me know, okay? I can't have my baby daughter living like this. I can help."

I shook my head. "I don't need your money."

He backed up. "Okay, then. I was just trying to be nice. Geez."

"Don't. I can take care of myself."

He lifted both his hands resignedly. "Okay, then. Guess I'll just leave. I'll pick her up tomorrow and take her to preschool. Cool?"

I nodded, biting back my emotions. So much was going through my mind at that moment. Matt being nice to me made me like him even though I didn't want to. I reminded myself that Matt was with another woman now, and I had thrown away my chance with him. It was my own decision, and I had to stick with it.

"That's cool, yes."

With Angel in my arms, I walked inside and closed the door behind me with a deep exhale. My sixteen-year-old daughter, Christine, stood by the window and watched Matt leave.

"Why is it that the two of you aren't together again?"

I grimaced and put Angel down so she could rush to her toys in the living room.

"It's complicated," I said. "Let's leave it at that."

"Doesn't seem that complicated to me," she said and walked by me with a sassy look, eating the rest of the Oreos from the kitchen.

Chapter 3

THEN:

It wasn't a bad neighborhood when they moved in at first. The Spanish house that Janet and Rob Carey bought just after they got married was the house of their dreams. It was the biggest one in the neighborhood, and they named it *the Mansion*. This was where their dreams of building a family would come true. There was no doubt.

Janet touched her bulging stomach gently as they walked around in the kitchen, lit up by the light from the sun rising behind the tall trees in the backyard—the very backyard where their children would have a swing set and maybe even a tree house.

Janet smiled when imagining it.

"What are you giggling about?" Rob asked, coming up from behind her, putting his arms around her neck, and pulling her into a hug.

She exhaled happily. "Nothing. Just... I'm just so happy right now."

"Me too, my love. I can't wait to stand here and watch our children play in the yard," he said.

Her smile grew wider. "I was just thinking the same thing."

"Well, great minds think alike," he said, kissing her neck. Janet had put her long blonde hair in a bun, so she wouldn't sweat so much. It was hot outside as summer approached, and the pregnancy made her feel so hot all the time. She liked being pregnant but was ready to hold her baby in her arms now. She was getting tired, and her feet were so swollen that she could only wear flip-flops these days. The baby kicked just as Rob placed his hand on her stomach.

"Uh, I felt that," he said with a huge grin. "That was a huge one."

"He's getting big. It's almost like there isn't room for him in there anymore," she said with that mild laughter that Rob found endearing. She was so beautiful to him right at that moment, when standing there in their house, all pregnant and big, the sunlight hitting her hair.

God, she was stunning.

How did he get so lucky?

He still didn't believe it.

"So, what do you say? Should we hang the big painting your mom gave us above the fireplace or by the dining table?"

She turned to face him. "I thought you hated that painting?"

"Yeah, well, I do, but I figured it means a lot to you since you and your mom are so close, so…."

She stopped him by kissing him, closing her eyes. Her lips felt so silky smooth against his that his knees grew soft. Janet had that effect on him just by entering a room. His heart would literally beat faster, and his breathing became ragged. That's how pretty she was.

"I love you, you silly man," she said with a soft smile as their lips parted. He could barely breathe when looking into her deep blue eyes.

"You make me so happy," he said and placed a hand on his beating heart. He was feeling emotional and almost tearing up.

"We're going to be so happy in this house. All of us. Together."

Chapter 4

"WHAT'S WITH THE DEEP SIGHS?"

I didn't look up at my mom but kept scrolling on my laptop, sitting in the kitchen while she was doing the dishes. She had come over for dinner to hang out with me and my kids, and my sister Sydney was there too. I had ordered in, so they cleaned up while I was sweating over my many bills piling up.

"Yeah, we've been listening to you make that noise ever since we left the table," Sydney said. She was trying to wipe off a pan but doing a bad job of it. She wasn't exactly used to doing domestic work as she had been a celebrity actress, or movie star, if you will, for most of her adult life until she met me and decided to give back to the world by building a shelter for trafficked women. Our dad had kidnapped her when we were just children, and we had grown up apart but recently reconnected. I loved having her in my life again.

"What's going on?"

I exhaled again and leaned back in the chair, then forced a smile.

"And there it is again," my mom said.

"Will you leave me alone? It's nothing," I said. "Just stuff."

"What kind of stuff?" my sister asked. "Must be pretty annoying stuff for you to make that face."

I chuckled and shook my head, then closed the lid of my computer. "It's nothing worth ruining our evening over. Is there any more Chardonnay?"

My sister dangled the bottle, and I went to get it. As I reached for it, she pulled it away.

"Not until you tell us what's going on."

"Oh, come on. What are we, ten?" I said and reached for it again, but she lifted it high, and since she was the height of a supermodel, and I most certainly wasn't, I couldn't reach it. I growled, annoyed.

"Mo-o-om?"

My mom burst into laughter, then put away the plate she had been drying. "You're on your own there, my sweet child," she said.

I stomped my feet like my toddler would. "Give it to me."

Sydney shook her head. "Not until you tell me what's going on. You never share anything with us. If you're in trouble, then I would like to know."

I sighed, aggravated, making sure she knew this bothered me. "All right. If you must know, I need new windows for the house. And I need a new door in the back, and maybe all new electricity. And it's a lot of money that I don't have right now. This year's last two hurricanes destroyed this old house, and I'm trying to find money for it. Okay, there, happy? Now, hand me the bottle."

Sydney lowered her hand, and I pulled it out of her grip. I poured myself the last glass, then sipped it. Both women stared at me.

"Why didn't you say something?" Sydney said. "I can help you. How much do you need?"

I almost choked on my wine, then shook my head.

"NO!"

She stared at me, eyes wide.

"What do you mean, *no?*"

"See, this is why I never tell you anything like this."

"Because I can help you?"

"Yes! Exactly. Because I knew you'd offer me the money, and I don't want your money."

"So, my money isn't good enough for you? Well, excuse me for wanting to help."

I scoffed. "Yeah, well, I… I just…."

She made a face, then looked at our mom. "I'm gonna go. I'm not wanted here."

I felt my heart rate go up. I loved my sister and didn't want her to go. Yet I didn't tell her. Instead, I stupidly said, "Yeah, you just go ahead and leave. It's what you do when things get rough, right? You always take the easy way out."

She gave me a strange look. "What is that supposed to mean?"

I couldn't look her in the eyes, so I turned away. "Nothing. Just that you always had it so easy, and I had to struggle throughout my entire life; that's all."

"Well, excuse me for trying to make your life a little easier," she said, grabbing her purse. She rushed to the door, then stopped. "And excuse me for being the one who was kidnapped when you weren't."

And just like that, she slammed the door. My mom stared at me, hands at her sides.

"What?" I asked.

"That was uncalled for."

"It's the truth. She thinks she can just come here and flaunt her lifestyle and money at me and make me feel like I'm worthless. But I'm not having it. I'll find a way to make this money on my own."

"How about that TV show that keeps calling you?"

It was my daughter, Christine, who had walked into the kitchen. "Sorry, I was watching TV," she said, "and you're being very loud."

"What TV show?" my mom asked, stepping forward.

I shook my head. "Nothing, Mom. It's nothing."

I made eyes at Christine to make her stop talking, but that didn't help. She continued unabated, "There's this TV show, some true-crime reality show filming down in Miami this month, and they want Mom to come and be on it. It's a new concept where they try to solve cases while being filmed. They've gotten like twenty-five million dollars from a network to do it, and if she's good, they might use her for other shows. They said they'd pay her and everything— like a lot. I think it sounds so cool."

I was shaking my head and making eyes at my daughter, letting her know she was dead meat. It didn't work. She shrugged and turned around, then walked back to her TV, and *Below Deck*, the reality show about people living and working on yachts.

"So, why aren't we taking this gig?" my mom asked.

"Please, don't say gig," I said and sat down with my wine. I sipped it again. "And it's just not for me, okay?"

"Why not, might I ask?"

"I just… I don't want that kind of attention, okay? I'm not some reality TV personality wanting the world to look at me, prepared to humiliate myself for money. I like privacy."

My mom tilted her head. "You might not want that kind of attention, but you do want that kind of money, don't you?"

"I don't care about the money. It's just not for me."

My mom threw the dishtowel on the counter, then turned to look at me, pointing a finger at me.

"You know what I think?"

"I really don't want to."

"I think you're a snob. You think you're too good for that TV show because you're a snob. There, I said it. Now, hate me."

She turned around, grabbed her car keys and purse from the counter, and gave me one last triumphant look before leaving my house.

I stared at the door after it had closed, then shook my head and returned to staring at my screen and the many numbers that wouldn't add up.

Chapter 5

"WHO HAD THE VEGGIE BURGER?"

Tara looked at the three others in the hotel suite. The TV crew had rented it for them to stay in while doing the recordings. It had two bedrooms. The girls slept in one and the boys in the other. It was evening now, and they were done for the day. They were all exhausted, so they had decided to order room service.

"I did."

Mike lifted his hand, and Tara was about to hand it to him.

"No, you didn't," Kim said.

"What?"

"You didn't get the veggie burger. I did."

"Excuse me?" Mike asked. "I think I know what I ordered. That burger is mine, and you know it."

"You got it wrong," Kim continued. "You had the burrito, remember? You couldn't decide between the two. You initially decided on the veggie burger but then changed your mind at the last minute. How do you not remember this? It was literally half an hour ago?"

Mike stared at her, then scoffed. "Well, excuse me for forgetting. It's not like it's that important."

"It is to me," Kim said, grabbing the burger from Tara's hand. "This is my burger."

"God, you're so… so…," Mike said, clutching his hands. He was speaking through gritted teeth.

"So, what?" Kim asked.

"So darn annoying and controlling."

"And you're a liar," she said with a huff. She sat down with the burger and started to unwrap it. She looked at it between her hands, then bit into it before she continued. "Just like your mother."

Mike rose to his feet.

"Excuse me? What did you just say?"

He stepped toward her, eyes sizzling in anger. She ignored him and continued to eat.

"That you're a liar just like your mom. My dad always said that your mom was probably the reason they got themselves into trouble if anyone was. Because you couldn't trust her."

Mike's nostrils were flaring, and his hands were in fists, his knuckles turning white. Scott got up and blocked his way, then pushed him back.

"Get out of my way."

But Scott didn't move. He stared at Mike and held his hand up to stop him. Scott was bigger than Mike, so he knew he didn't stand a chance.

"Easy there, tiger," Scott said. "No need to do something you might regret later. Fighting isn't the answer, and you know it. Don't forget. We're all here for the same reason."

"I'm here because it's a good career move," Kim said, lifting her nose toward the ceiling.

"How is this a career move?" Mike asked.

"I want to be in reality TV, and this will give me experience and make me a known face. I've always been told I have a good face for TV. That's why I'm doing it. I don't know why any of you are here."

Mike growled, and Scott pushed him back again.

"It's not worth it," Scott said. "Back down."

He did. He returned to his chair and his burrito, then started eating, not even looking at Kim. Tara felt her heart rate go down again. She had been so worried they'd get into a fight. It could ruin everything for them. The whole premise for the TV show was the united front of them helping each other find out what happened to their mothers, not fighting over whose fault it was that they never came back—or for them to become TV stars either.

It was so ridiculous.

She looked at the pizza slice in front of her but had lost her appetite. She spotted Scott as he went out on the balcony, and she followed him, then closed the sliding door behind her. Scott was vaping while leaning on the railing overlooking the many lights covering the city of Miami. They could see the ocean from their balcony. It was beautiful.

"Are you okay?" she asked, standing next to him. She looked down at the street below, then felt dizzy at the thought of how far up they were. The view was great from this height, but she wouldn't want to be the one to fall.

He blew out smoke, then put the vape back to his mouth and huffed a few times. "Yeah, I'm fine. I just really don't want to be here. I don't see what good can come of this. The police gave up a long time ago. Why do they think we can figure anything out?"

"I heard they tried to get this famous FBI profiler to help, but I think she said no."

"See? We're the only ones stupid enough to buy into this. I should never have agreed to it. It was a mistake. I can't stop feeling like it was a huge mistake."

Tara looked at Scott. She had loved him for as long as she could remember. Maybe she had said yes to this show because it might bring her closer to him. Was that why? It was a part of it, at least. Did she really believe the TV show could accomplish anything?

Probably not.

"Well, tomorrow, they're taking us to the club where our mothers were seen partying and dancing on the night when they disappeared," she said. "Maybe that will feel like some sort of closure. At least, I'm hoping it will. That's why I'm here—to get closure."

It was a lie, and she knew it. But hopefully, Scott didn't. Hopefully, he wouldn't be able to look into her eyes and see the huge crush on him that she tried so painfully hard to suppress.

Scott smiled, accepting her answer and she was relieved, though a little guilty. She had never lied to him before, but then again, she had never felt like this before either. She could only hope that he wouldn't find out the truth.

Because that would just about kill her.

Chapter 6

MATT BROUGHT his new girlfriend when he picked up Angel the next day to take her to preschool. She was sitting in the car, and he got out. I knew who she was and had met her once when he presented her to me one day. So, I waved politely, and she waved back, even though it seemed a little uncomfortable for her. She was like fifteen years younger than Matt and very intimidated by the fact that he had children.

"She's pretty even in the mornings, huh?" I said with an awkward smile as he approached me. Angel held onto me tightly as she saw her dad's arms reach for her. She turned her back on him with a grunt.

"She's been a little moody this morning," I said, handing him the bag first. She was going to his house after preschool today and staying the night, so I had packed all the necessities.

He grabbed it and looked at me. I glanced at the woman in his car. "So... how are things with her?"

He shrugged. "They're pretty good."

"I bet. She's beautiful."

"Yeah, you said that. Listen, I'm in a rush this morning. Come here, baby girl; Daddy is going to take you to preschool."

He reached for her again, but she hugged me tighter and shook her head. I sighed. "Sweetie, Daddy will take you to see Miss Mimi, and maybe she will let you play with the crayons today. How about that?"

That didn't help. Matt looked frustratedly at his watch. "I have a meeting at nine. I need to go."

I was about to make a joke about his girlfriend, Elyse, and going to preschool, but I held it back. I tried to hand over Angel, but she refused.

"Come on, sweetie," Matt said. "Come to Daddy?"

She looked at him with a sniffle, then changed her mind. She smiled and reached for him, and he grabbed her in his arms. Then, he laughed as she hugged him tightly. That made me laugh too.

Why was this so hard? Why couldn't we just be a family?

He walked to the car, put her in her seat, and then slammed the door.

"By the way. What's this I hear about a TV show?"

My eyes grew wide. "Where did you hear about that?"

He shrugged. "Your mom told me."

"My mom?"

"Yeah, we talk from time to time. I was always her favorite, remember?"

I rolled my eyes. "How could I forget?"

"But you're not doing it?"

I shook my head. "No."

He paused, keys dangling in his hand. A wrinkle grew between his eyes. "Why not?"

"Because I don't want to."

"But you need the money?"

"Not that bad."

"I think you should do it."

"Okay, but that's not gonna make me want to." I waved at Angel in her car seat. I hated saying goodbye to her in the mornings, knowing I wouldn't see her until the next day. It was the worst.

"It's good money and exposure. I don't understand," he continued.

I gave him a look to cut it out. "No, it's not."

"You've written books. This might help spike sales?"

"Maybe, but I don't want to do it. End of story. Now, weren't you in a hurry? To a meeting?"

He cleared his throat. "How about if I go with you?"

"What?"

"Yeah, we've been a team before. Remember? We've worked together solving cases."

I shook my head violently, letting him know I believed he had gone completely mad. I lifted my finger.

"Oh, no, no."

"Why not? I'm a detective. Plus, I did a little TV in college, remember? I told you about it."

"I really don't think that will help me, but thanks."

"Do it," Matt said. "It might be fun or interesting."

"It will be neither. Just annoying. And painful. Trust me."

"Come on. Don't say no to an opportunity like this. I will be there and help you with anything you need."

That made me laugh. He looked at me like he didn't understand my reaction.

"We will fight all day."

He threw out his arms. "TV shows love that. Listen, I will do this just to help you out. I won't take any of the money; you're the one they want, but I can help as your assistant."

I stared at him, unable to believe I was actually hearing these words coming from his mouth.

"You just want to be on TV, don't you?"

He nodded. "So, what if I do? Is that so wrong?"

"I don't believe you."

He growled. "So, you're really not going to do it?"

"Nope."

"Gosh, you're going to be the death of me. To pass on an opportunity like this? Who does that?"

I scoffed, then blew kisses at my daughter inside the car. She was crying now, as usual when saying goodbye to me. It tore my heart apart. I turned around and faced Matt again.

"I do."

I walked past him toward the door and heard him sigh, annoyed, behind me. I decided to ignore it.

Chapter 7

THEN:

After having their fourth child and seeing her off to school, Janet Carey started to get bored alone at home. She didn't want a full-time job, which would keep her away from her children too much, and they still needed her. She became a music teacher at the local school. This way, she saw her children during the day, and she could combine working with her love of both children and music. She only worked three days a week; the rest she spent taking care of the house and the family while Rob handled his job at the insurance company.

It was a dream situation for them both.

Janet also soon joined the local choir at the Baptist church and would spend hours at the piano at the house, playing while the kids were in school, rehearsing for the coming Sunday's sermon. At dinner, she quoted scripture for the kids, and they would sing songs to praise Him.

She could sit for hours on the back porch watching the kids play in the yard, her heart full of joy and gratitude for how blessed she was.

On Fridays, she would usually grocery shop and bake cookies that the kids enjoyed when coming home from school.

This Friday was no different.

At least not to begin with.

Janet had just stowed away all the groceries and closed the garage door. She went to the kitchen and found all the ingredients she needed for her cookies. She decided to put raisins in them for a change—to make them healthier than the usual chocolate ones, but then changed her mind again and put the raisins back. Who was she kidding? She didn't even like cookies with raisins in them. Why would the children?

Smiling secretively to herself, she grabbed the chocolate instead and left the pantry. She put together the dough and placed the cookies on the baking sheet, making sure to make them all the same size, so no one would fight over the bigger ones. She usually saved one for Rob, too, in a place the children couldn't reach. She would give it to him once he got home late, as usual, on Fridays and tell him to keep it a secret from the children.

She opened the oven, put the cookies inside, then closed it and set the timer. Then she looked at her phone and sighed, a little annoyed. The plumber had said he would stop by today, but she hadn't heard from him. The toilet in the back room was clogged, and they hadn't been able to use it all week. If he didn't come today, she knew very well it would have to wait until after the weekend. Why was it always like that when you needed the help of a handyman?

She called him but got his voicemail and left a message. He was probably attending to an emergency somewhere, and maybe he would get there afterward.

Yes, she had to believe he would be there when he had promised to.

Janet turned on the TV and watched the news for a few minutes while waiting for the cookies to be done, then got bored with all the bad news and switched the channel. She found some crime show that got her hooked right away, and she couldn't stop watching, even after she had taken the cookies out of the oven. Halfway through it, she heard the doorbell ring, and—thinking it had to be the plumber, finally—she got up and rushed to open the door.

Chapter 8

I LOGGED into my bank app and closed my eyes, not daring to see what it said. I took a few deep breaths, then finally found the courage to open them and look. Then my heart sank. It wasn't good.

I decided to close it again, then grabbed some more coffee. I looked over the canal in my backyard and spotted a grey heron on my dock. The wood had taken a bad beating during the last storm, and some of the planks had fallen into the water. I had told my kids not to use the dock until we got it fixed, but now it seemed like the last thing on my long *to-be-done* list.

How was I going to afford to stay in this house?

I sipped from my cup while wondering what to do. Should I just swallow my pride and take money from my sister? But how would I ever pay her back? She would end up resenting me, and I would resent myself because of it. It would become this thing between us that we didn't talk about, but both knew it was there.

No, there was no way I could do that.

Would I be forced to sell my home?

I couldn't bear the thought. I had four children. Where would we live? With my mom?

The very thought made me shiver.

I finished my coffee, then put the cup in the sink while looking at the long-legged bird in my backyard. I loved this house and had re-found my love for this beach town I grew up in. I really didn't want to have to move.

I opened my laptop and sat at the kitchen table, then scrolled through available jobs that I might take. I knew I could be of use somewhere, right? But it had to be well paid, or I would never make enough for what I needed. And none of the available jobs came near what I needed.

I closed the lid and spotted the mailman as he drove up to my mailbox. I walked out there and took the mail, then went back inside, flipping through mostly spam letters and pamphlets from real estate agents wanting to sell my house. I looked at one smiling at me and considered him for a minute, then continued going through them. And then I stopped. The next letter was from Brevard Surgical Center. Alex had to have his tonsils removed a few months earlier, and I had paid almost a thousand dollars out of pocket against my deductible, but they said the insurance would pay the rest. As I read through the letter, I realized the insurance company had only paid a few hundred dollars.

I had to pay the rest.

My heart skipped a beat as I looked at the numbers. I felt my cheeks begin to flush, and I could barely breathe. This was a lot of money—money I didn't have.

I sat down on my couch, pulling my hair in frustration.

There really was no other way out, was there?

I sighed and growled, annoyed, then grabbed my phone and called Matt.

"Get packing."

"Really? We're doing it?"

"Don't sound so excited."

I hung up, then called my mom.

"I need you to take care of my children. Your daughter is about to become a TV star."

She shrieked on the other end. "Really? I… I can't believe it."

"Easy now, Mom, that was a joke. No one is becoming a star here. I'm only in it for the money."

She told me she could take the kids as long as needed, and I hung up, then called the producer, who had been calling and emailing me several times a week for the past few months. I took a deep breath before saying the words, "I'm in."

Chapter 9

"IN THIS CLUB behind me that we will enter in a few minutes, we know, according to the police reports, that all four mothers, Kristen Thomasson, Pat Baxter, Janice Howard, and Marley Lamar were partying, drinking, and dancing until the early morning hours. What happened to them after they visited this club remains a mystery. Did they get drugged and kidnapped? Did they get into a fight and kill each other? Or did they simply just decide to run away, all four of them together, and are they now living somewhere in the Caribbean? That's what we're here to help their children find out. We know that earlier in the day, they had gone to a spa to get their nails done and have massages, and then they ended up partying here in this club."

Barbara paused and looked at Billy, who raised a finger to signal he had gotten it all. Her face changed from fake smiling to frustration, and she lowered the microphone in her hand.

"How was that? Was it okay?" she asked Billy. "I feel that it wasn't. Did I use the same phrase twice? I said in this club three times, didn't I?"

Lydia, the producer standing behind Billy, approached her. "You did, but I don't think the viewers will notice."

Barbara sighed. "Maybe I should do it again, just to be sure."

"If that will make you feel better, then let's do that," Lydia said, signaling Billy. She rolled her eyes as she turned around and faced Billy. He smiled.

"By all means, let's do a fifteenth take," she mumbled when walking up behind him. She smiled and signaled to Barbara to start whenever she was ready.

Barbara did the take once more and finally seemed satisfied. Then the producer signaled the four teenagers to come closer. Tara felt nervous, as she knew it was now their turn to perform.

"All right," Lydia said, looking each of them in the eyes to ensure she had their full attention. "Everyone knows what to do, right?"

Tara smiled nervously. She knew, but she wasn't sure she would be able to do it well enough.

"We have a couple of extra cameras on you today to ensure we get you from all angles, but pay no attention to them, okay?" Lydia said. "Just walk in there and do your thing; pretend you're looking for answers, and don't be afraid to show us your emotions. Emotions make good television."

It was a sentence she used a lot, Tara thought. Making good television. What did that even mean?

"So, do we all walk in at once?" Kim asked. "And what are we supposed to feel when we go in there? I need some coaching on that."

"You two walk in first, and then Tara and Scott will come after," Lydia said. "And just be real, like surprised or feeling sad. This is where your moms spent their last night, remember?"

"We don't know that," Scott added. "We don't know that they're dead."

"You're right; I'm sorry about that," Lydia said, hugging her iPad against her chest. She clung to that thing like her life depended on it. It held everything in it that she needed, Scott had told Tara. And he called it the script. Tara didn't understand that since it was supposed to be a reality show they were filming. What was there to script? But Scott had told her that she was naïve if she thought it wasn't somehow planned out.

"It's all scripted," he had said. "Even our freaking emotions."

Tara didn't understand how that was possible. Yet as she walked up to the club entrance and noticed Lydia whispering extra instructions to Kim, she couldn't escape the feeling that maybe Scott was onto something.

Chapter 10

THE DRIVE DOWN to Miami was unbearable. Matt was in the best mood, whistling loudly in the car, while I was regretting my decision repeatedly and stress eating M&M's, feeling awful about myself. I had been doing so well lately but couldn't stay off the junk anymore. It wasn't exactly the best timing since I was about to appear on TV, and we all know the camera adds some pounds. But at this point, I couldn't care anymore. I needed something to help me calm down, and this was my addiction.

"Could you not, please?" I said as we reached Ft. Lauderdale. We had just passed the Hard Rock Hotel, which was shaped like a guitar.

"Could I not... what?" he asked, confused.

"Whistle," I said. "It's annoying."

"Okay," he said, looking out the window while his fingers drummed on his knees.

"Sorry," I said. "I'm being a jerk. I'm just nervous. It's not exactly my cup of tea what we're about to do."

"It's okay," he said with a grin. "Luckily, I love this stuff."

"Maybe you can brief me a little on the case. You got the files, right? I've read through them, but maybe something will jump out at me if you go through it as well."

"Sure," he said, grabbing his laptop from the back seat. He opened the lid and started typing. "All right. So, we have four women, all in their late thirties to early forties; they went missing three years ago on a trip to Miami. They're all from the same little town called Russell Springs in Kentucky. They knew each other from their mother's group, and all had a child that was fifteen years old, eighteen now. It's those kids that the TV show people found and want to do the show about."

"Yes, about them finding the truth or getting closure, whatever that is," I added.

"Wow. You really don't like this type of TV, do you?" he asked.

I sighed. "I haven't watched much of it, I have to admit. But just the term reality TV makes my skin crawl."

"But this is a new type of show, as I understand it. And it sounds kind of cool," he said. "Solving cases on live TV."

"It's not live TV," I said with a chuckle. "It's everything but."

"But it's real and rough, right?"

I shook my head. "I find it hard to believe. I think they have an entire script, and we all just need to fill out our roles."

"But surely they can't script whether or not we solve the case?" he asked.

I sighed and passed a truck. "I wouldn't be so sure."

"Why can't you just devote yourself to this? Make the most of it?"

"It's just hard for me," I said. "What else do you have?"

He looked back at the screen. "They were all at a club dancing and seen leaving there at around two-thirty in the morning. A camera caught them from behind and showed a man with them, but no one has ever been able to identify who he was. That's when they were last seen. No one has heard anything from them since, and it remains a mystery where they went after the club. They never returned to their hotel that night. Their phones and credit cards were all found in a garbage bag behind a Seven-Eleven not far from the club. Unfortunately, no cameras caught them being thrown out. And they were never able to turn on the phones and get information from them as they had gotten water in them, probably from the rain."

"But that does tell a story," I said. "I just don't know which one."

"You think they were kidnapped?"

"I don't really know. Or maybe they all decided to leave their lives behind?"

"That's a possibility," he said. "I mean, you always hear these stories about someone walking out to get cigarettes and never coming back. That type of thing? You're thinking that now they're all sitting on some island somewhere? I could totally see that."

"It just doesn't fit with their descriptions. According to their families, they were all devoted mothers," I said. "Not one suffered from depression or even seemed tired of their lives. One of them, Pat, had a dispute with her ex about custody, so I could maybe see her doing something like that, but wouldn't she take the kid with her?"

I took the exit toward Miami and found the right street to get to the hotel that the producer had us staying in. I couldn't stop seeing the pictures of the four women in my mind, the one taken of them all together as they went to dinner the night they disappeared. Pat had posted it on her Facebook page under the caption, "We are never going home." If only she had known how right she was. It was almost eerie that she would write something like that.

I stopped the car in front of the hotel, then looked at Matt. "I say we focus our energy on solving this case and helping their families find out what really happened. *That* I can devote myself to."

Chapter 11

"Yes?"

Janet stared at the man outside her door. He didn't look much like a plumber. No shirt with a company logo, toolbox, or anything indicated he was there to do work.

"Are you here to look at the toilet?" she asked, still hoping that's why he was there, still thinking he had to be the plumber.

Why else would he ring her doorbell?

The man's dark eyes stared at her from beneath the blue cap. The look in them made her feel uncomfortable. Immediately, she pulled back and tried to close the door, but the man placed a hand on it and pushed it.

Janet flew back into the wall behind her, knocking down a flower vase from the small table. She shrieked as she watched the man enter the house, slamming the door behind him. She tried to get up but placed her hand on a piece of the broken vase and cut herself.

"Ouch," she cried and looked at it. It was bleeding. She tried to get up once again, but the man moved swiftly. He towered over her, then grabbed her by the hair and pulled it. Janet screamed in panic and fear while he pulled her across the old Spanish tiles and threw her on the floor. Then, he leaned over her and slammed his fist into her face.

Janet screamed.

"Please. Don't… I have money. Cash."

He punched her again, and Janet screamed.

"Please, stop!"

He then grabbed her around the neck and started to choke her. Janet gurgled and begged for her life while barely able to breathe.

"Take… everything… you… want."

His eyes fell on her wedding ring—the one with the big diamond Rob's grandmother had brought when escaping Germany during the war. It had been the only thing of value she was able to bring, and it had been handed down through the family for many years. Janet was planning on one day giving it to her firstborn son to give to his wife.

"No… no… not… the ring. Please, it's an heirloom, it's a family…."

The man didn't listen. He grabbed the ring and pulled it off her finger hard. Janet screamed while he held her down by sitting on her, his knee pressed against her throbbing chest.

The ring came off, and the man looked at it in the light, then grinned. He put it in his pocket.

"What else do you got, huh?"

She shook her head. "Nothing. I'm not rich. We don't have anything."

"Your wallet. Where's your wallet?"

She lifted a finger and pointed at her purse that had also fallen from the small table when she knocked over the vase. It was on the tiles. The man saw it, let go of Janet, and sprang for it. He opened the wallet, then looked at her.

"That's it? Twenty bucks?"

"I'm… sorry… I don't have more."

He reached into the purse and pulled out her car keys. "I'll take this one, too, then."

At this point, Janet didn't care anymore what he took—as long as he let her live. He came up to her, keys dangling in his hand, then punched her again.

Janet screamed. "Please… I have children."

The man paused. Then he grabbed the vacuum cleaner standing in the foyer and pulled out the cord. He used it to tie her up and placed a folded sock in her mouth. Then, he kicked her one last time before he left.

Chapter 12

BEING at the club and talking to the bartender who had served her mother that night was a lot for Tara. From what he told them, she barely recognized the woman who had been her mother. She sounded more like a wild teenager going on a rager—the way he described them dancing on the bar counter and taking off their tops so they only wore bras.

Was that really her mother?

He said they had been doing shots toward the end of the night. Tequila, and after that, they left. All four of them together, he said.

"But I did sense that there was tension between the two of them. The tall blonde one and the short brown-haired one," he said. "I heard them fight over something here at the bar right before they left. The tall blonde called the other a *liar* and told her to *stop judging* her. Whatever that meant."

That had to be Pat and Marley. Just like their children, Mike and Kim, they didn't do well together. They probably couldn't stand one another.

"Did they seem upset when they left?" Barbara asked while Billy filmed the conversation from over her shoulder, getting a closeup of the bartender's reaction to her question.

He paused and thought for a second. "Now that you mention it, yes. I think that's why they left. The third woman came up to those two and asked them to stop and said, '*We're leaving now. You're too drunk, and that's when you fight.*' Something like that."

Probably Janice, Scott's mom, Tara thought to herself. She had often been described as the mother of the group, the one who took care of the others. She had told them it was time to go home.

Then why didn't they?

Tara felt her heart rate go up and felt a deep overwhelming nausea rush through her body. It was like the room was spinning, and she rushed outside, where she threw up on the sidewalk. When she was done, she looked up and saw Billy with the camera, filming her as she wiped her mouth with her sleeve.

Kim hurried over to her. "Are you okay?"

Tara scoffed, knowing Kim was only doing this for the sake of the camera. But she decided to play along and nodded. "Yeah, I'm fine. It was just a little overwhelming."

"Our next stop is the place where they found the phones in a trash bag," Barbara said, coming out of the club. "I say we start walking the same way they did, and we should reach it in a few minutes."

Tara felt slightly sick again at the thought of being confronted with more of this type of stuff, but this was what she had signed up for, and now there was no way back.

With cameras rolling, they began to walk down the sidewalk, the same way their mothers had, side by side, backs turned to the club and the security footage that had captured the last moments of their mothers' night before their disappearance. It felt odd to walk like this, but Barbara wanted it that way.

It was apparently considered good television.

They walked down the sidewalk, all in silence, feeling all kinds of emotions, including awkwardness. Kim lifted her nose toward the sky and strutted while sticking out her behind, walking in a weird manner that didn't look very natural but probably was considered hot.

Tara didn't pay her much attention. She could see the Seven-Eleven sign in the distance, and as they approached it, she felt her hands grow clammy. Her breathing became ragged, and she felt dizzy.

This was it. This trash bin they were heading toward had contained the last sign of life they had of their mothers. Somehow, all their phones and credit cards had ended up in this bin inside the same trash bag, among hotdog leftovers and empty soda bottles. But why? And how?

Was it something they deliberately did to ensure no one could track them?

Or had they been taken from them involuntarily?

That was the big question here.

Tara breathed heavily as they approached the bin. Barbara stopped, then signaled Billy to come behind her and continue to film. She looked at each of them, and they at her.

"This is it, kiddos," she said. "The last tracks of your mothers ended here. This is the last thing the police found. Their belongings were in a bag in this bin. How does that make you feel?"

"I, for one, am super emotional right now," Kim said and fake cried a little. It was to be expected, and Tara welcomed it. When Kim took the stage, she didn't have to.

Kim continued with a loud sniffle and pretended to be doing everything she could to hold back her tears. "To think that this is the last trace of my mom is quite… it's very overwhelming."

Kim paused. She stopped crying and then said, "No, wait. That was the wrong word; can we do that again?"

Barbara let her. While Kim did her thing for the camera, Tara walked away from the group to take a break. She found it hard to breathe properly with all these people surrounding her constantly, and she felt very emotional—like for real emotional, not like Kim-emotional.

She was about to cry.

She just didn't want it on camera. It was private for her. She snuck around the corner of the Seven-Eleven and leaned on the wall, shutting out the noise and Kim's annoying voice in the distance. She closed her eyes and breathed deeply a few times to calm herself, then opened them again.

And that was when she saw it.

At first, she didn't think it was anything important. But as she stared at the many black birds pecking at the dirt on the empty lot next to the gas station, she got curious. This wasn't the first animal that had dug in that area, she realized as she approached it. The grass had been ripped open and dirt dug up. The birds were scared away as she came closer but stayed close. Some of them circled above her head, waiting for her to go away so they could return to whatever it was. Their wings were beating the air around her, and the flapping of their wings created a soft whip-like sound. Tara stared down at the thing on the ground, a shiver running through her.

It was a bone.

Tara had been taking biology in school long enough to know that it was way too big to belong to an animal.

It was a human bone.

Part II

TWO HOURS LATER

Chapter 13

"WHAT DO you mean your mom isn't coming for Thanksgiving this year?"

Joe Fischer looked at his wife, Allyssa, with a slight shrug. She stared at him, waiting for his answer. He had just come home from work and was going through the mail. He was still in his suit but had loosened the tie as he always did on his way home from the law firm.

"I don't know. I think it means that she isn't coming?"

But...," Allyssa complained. "We always have Thanksgiving together."

Joe sighed. "And we always end up fighting. Maybe this year we can have a quiet one with just you, me, and the kids."

"And your brother," she said with a deep exhale. She returned to peeling the potato in her hand.

"What's wrong with my brother now?" he asked.

"Nothing. He's just...."

Joe came up behind her and rubbed her shoulders, then kissed her neck. "I know he's a pothead—the black sheep of the family and all that. But he has nowhere else to go—no family other than us. And he loves the girls. They love him and always hang with him in the pool. They have fun together."

"Okay," Allyssa said. "But he can't show up high. If he does, you tell him to leave. And he can't smoke here either if that's what he's planning to do."

"Frankly, I think he's mostly doing edibles now," Joe said, taking off his suit jacket. He hung it on the back of a kitchen chair, opened the fridge, and pulled out a bottle of red wine.

"But still. Promise me that," she said. "I can't have him ruin everything or be around the children while being like that."

Joe opened the wine and smiled. "I promise I will have a talk with him."

She nodded, and Joe poured them each a glass. He handed it to her, and she sipped it. It felt good after a long day of raising children and doing chores. The girls drove her crazy from time to time, especially lately.

They clinked glasses. "To a wonderful Thanksgiving this year."

She smiled. "Easy for you to say. You don't have to cook it."

He nodded and drank from his glass. "You got me there. At least I will have some time off from Mrs. Valdez and her divorce."

"They still can't agree on the house, huh?"

He shook his head. "Don't remind me. What's for dinner?"

"Chicken. So, why did your mom say she wasn't coming again?" Allyssa asked, finishing the last potato.

He hesitated. "She didn't."

Allyssa looked at him. "You're a terrible liar."

He scoffed. "Okay, then. She said something about wanting to keep the family peace or something like that. I don't even know."

Allyssa nodded. The fight Joe and his mother had the year before had been quite harsh. If she was being honest, she was kind of relieved that his mother wasn't coming. The constant criticism she provided and the underlying anger issues they all had—it was a lot. But the girls did love their grandmother, and they would miss her. The French doors opened, and her stepdaughter, Sabrina, peeked in.

"Did you hear?"

"Hear what?" Joe asked.

Her eyes grew wide. "They found a body by the Seven-Eleven, close to the school, right by the last bus stop. There are police cars everywhere, and they blocked it all off. I'm gonna ride my bike down there and look."

"No. Don't go there. Stay away from that area," Joe said.

"Aw, but Daddy…!"

She gave him the begging eyes, but he didn't budge.

"I don't want you anywhere near it, you hear me?"

Her shoulders slumped, and she turned her back on them. "Okay, I guess."

Allyssa stared at him, and he shook his head. "Kids these days. As if a crime scene is some TV show."

Allyssa smiled and tilted her head. "Dinner should be ready in twenty minutes."

Chapter 14

"WHAT DO WE KNOW?"

I had parked the car across the street from the police blockage, and we both got out. The show's producer had called us just as we arrived at the hotel and told us to hurry downtown. Matt had then talked to the local police to get an update while I drove us down there to meet them.

"Not much so far," he said. "The TV crew was apparently filming in the area where they found the four women's phones and credit cards when one of the participants, a young girl, spotted something and realized it was a bone. The crew then called the police, and they blocked off the area. Forensics are here now, and they have set up tents and lights, planning on working all night."

"You must be Eva Rae Thomas. Welcome."

The small woman with short spiky hair shook my hand. She was holding an iPad with the other, clinging onto it so tight it looked like she was terrified someone might steal it.

"I'm Lydia. We spoke on the phone?"

I nodded. "You're Lydia, the one who has been my plague for these past few months."

She smiled. "I'm so happy we finally managed to convince you to come. We could really use someone like you on this show—like permanently."

"Let's not get ahead of ourselves just yet," I said. "Let's see if I like it first."

She nodded. "Of course. Of course."

She signaled a big bearded guy with a camera to come closer. "This is Billy. He will be filming, documenting everything you do."

"Hi, Billy."

He gave me a thumbs-up.

"And these are the children."

Four teenagers about the same age as my oldest came forward. I greeted each of them.

"This is Tara, Scott, Mike, and Kim."

They didn't seem enthusiastic about meeting me. To be honest, they were all a little pale, except for Kim, who smiled widely and gave me a big hug.

"Okay, then," I said as she wrapped her arms around me. "That's what we're doing then?"

"I'm just so happy you're here," she said. "I've heard so much about you, and I feel confident that you can help us find out the truth about what really happened to our mothers."

She glanced at the camera to ensure it got everything, then walked away from me. "So… you're filming everything we do?" I asked.

Lydia nodded. "Yes, most of it will be edited out, but we want to document the entire process of solving this case."

"Now, I haven't promised you that I can actually solve it," I said. "Let's just make this clear. I'll do my best, but there are no guarantees."

"Of course not. We're mostly interested in the process here. And the emotional journey of the teenagers, of course."

I nodded. "I see." I glanced at Matt and then at the camera that already annoyed me the way it was following my every move, constantly in my face. "Let's get to work then, shall we?"

Chapter 15

Rob ran a red light and then a stop sign. He turned right and drove onto his street, the car skidding sideways. He spotted the two police cars when he drove up toward his house, heart throbbing in his throat.

He had been in a meeting when they called. His secretary had interrupted them and told him he had an important call. It was the police.

Rob threw the car onto the side of the road, then hurried up the driveway, where a uniformed police officer stopped him.

"You can't go in there, sir."

"It's my house. I'm Rob Carey; my wife is in there. Is she...?"

The officer's facial expression changed drastically when realizing who he was. He moved to the side and out of his way.

"Go ahead."

Rob ran past him and to the open door, then stepped inside. A photographer was taking pictures, and they were dusting for fingerprints.

"My wife," he said. "Janet. Where is she?"

A police officer approached him. "Are you Rob Carey?"

He nodded, biting back the fear. "Y-yes, that's me. What happened?"

"I'm sorry to have to tell you this, but your daughter came home from school and walked in to find your wife on the floor, tied up with a cord from a vacuum cleaner."

"A vacuum cleaner? What? I don't understand?"

"We believe she was the victim of a home invasion," he said with the same serious demeanor. "You know—some guy looking for cash and maybe jewelry that he can sell. Probably a drug addict looking to pay for his next fix."

Rob stared at the police officer without blinking. "Someone attacked my wife? And... and tied her up?"

"Yes. Your daughter was smart and called the police immediately. When the responding officers arrived, they found your wife in the foyer, bleeding on the floor."

"But... but she's alive?"

"Yes, she's in the kitchen right now while we wait for the ambulance. Your daughter is with her."

Rob turned on his heel and stormed to the kitchen, almost tripping over his own feet as he ran.

"Janet, Janet... oh, dear God," he said as he spotted her sitting on a kitchen chair. Her face was bruised, and she was bleeding from a wound on her forehead. She looked up at him.

"I'm okay, Rob."

"Daddy, Daddy," their daughter said and ran to him. She hugged him. "Oh, Daddy, it was so scary. Mom was covered with blood, and it was on the floor and on the walls too. It was really scary."

He hugged her back, feeling so much anger rising inside of him. To think that a young girl like her should have to experience that— finding her own mother like that. It was unbearable.

It was a nightmare.

"I'm so sorry, sweetie. I'm so, so sorry."

The police officer peeked inside. "The ambulance is here. They're bringing the stretcher in now."

"I'm scared, Daddy," his daughter said, clinging to him.

"It's gonna be okay, sweetie," he said while they put Janet on the stretcher and rolled her out. "First, they will take care of your mom, and then they will catch whoever did this to her. And then, he is going to jail for a very long time. Right, Officer?"

He looked at the police officer for assurance. The guy nodded slightly casually.

"Sure. We will do everything we can. I promise."

Chapter 16

"I CAN'T BELIEVE you found a body. An actual body."

Scott ran a hand through his curly hair in distress. He was pale and looked shocked. Tara felt the same way. She hadn't been able to get those images out of her mind—of the bones and the animals.

"I barely believe it either," she said.

They were back at the hotel inside their suite. Mike came out of his room, holding a small can in his hand.

"Who wants to do one with me? I think we need it."

"Edibles?" Kim said. "Phew, not me. I'm not jeopardizing my career by doing drugs."

"They're not exactly drugs," Scott said. "I'll do half of a gummy."

Tara looked at the can as it was passed around. Those tiny gummies looked so innocent. As it reached her, she paused.

"Take one," Mike said.

She looked up at him nervously.

"Have you never tried it before?" Scott asked.

She shook her head.

"It's okay. You don't have to."

"No. I want to," she said, and reached into them, grabbed a whole gummy, and ate it.

"Whoa, there," Scott said. "That's a lot when you've never tried it before."

"In her defense, she did just uncover a dead body today," Mike said, taking one himself. "I say she needs it."

Tara lay on the couch and looked at the ceiling. "Whose body do you think it was?"

They answered with silence. They all feared the same thing and had thought about it all afternoon, but no one dared to say it.

Could it be one of their mothers?

"It could be anyone," Mike said.

"But you have to admit, it was kind of random," Tara said and sat up. She was beginning to feel the effects of the gummy now. At least, she believed she was, but maybe it was just something she imagined. "That we'd find it right there, in the last place our moms were."

"Technically, we don't even know if they were there or if someone just dumped their phones and credit cards there," Mike added.

"True," she said. "But they were last seen walking in that direction."

Mike nodded. "Yeah. But that doesn't mean it was one of them."

"True," Tara said.

Kim sat down on the couch. She looked at them, and they looked at her.

"What?" Mike asked. "Why do you look so fishy?"

"I don't look *fishy*," she said, making a face. "Who says that anyway?"

"Why do you look so weird?" Scott asked.

That made Tara laugh. She held a hand to cover her mouth. It wasn't that funny; she knew it wasn't, but she just found it hilarious. Scott was so funny. He was so… so funny, and so…so….

"Well, there's something I haven't told you guys," Kim said. "Or anyone else, for that matter."

They all looked at her, anticipating what would come next. Not that any of them could prepare themselves for what did come next:

"You can't tell anyone, but this is not the last sign of life that was ever heard from them."

Chapter 17

"EVA RAE THOMAS! I'll be.... It's been a moment."

I smiled at my old colleague and friend, Tyler Fickle. He was head of the forensics department in Miami PD, and we had worked on several cases together when I was working with the FBI.

Tyler was a short, stubby bald white guy who carried most of his weight in his belly. He was also one of the nicest men I had ever met or worked with and one of the absolute best in his field. He was married to Anette, a tall blonde woman that always made heads turn when they entered a room together, and most people wondered how on earth a guy like him scored a woman like her. But they loved one another dearly, and the few times I had spent time with them, I had always been left with a hope that love can last after all and love can be enough.

He reached out his gloved hands, dirty from digging bones out of the ground. "I would give you a hug, but...."

"I'll pass," I said. I had put on gloves myself and plastic covers for my shoes. Matt had done the same and came up behind me.

"This is Matt," I said. "My... partner. He's a detective with CBPD."

Tyler gave me a look. "I heard you were back in that old sleepy town of yours. Nice to meet you, Matt."

Matt nodded in greeting. Billy, the cameraman, had been allowed to follow us in and had put plastic covers on his shoes as well. He snuck to the side and filmed. Tyler looked at me again.

"Don't mind him. We're doing some TV show, and the girl who found the bones is part of it. Do you mind if he films what you tell me?"

Tyler smiled happily. "Not at all. I've done a few TV shows myself in my career, so I know my way around. It's not my first rodeo if you catch my drift."

I smiled and nodded. Billy moved closer. He had put a microphone on me to get the sound. I kept accidentally hitting it with my hand.

"What have you got?" I asked.

Tyler went serious. "Come, take a look."

We knelt next to the body, and he showed us the bones they had found so far. They had dusted them and placed them in the pattern they believed they belonged, shaping what was undoubtedly a human body with the skull on top. Seeing this made it very real to me, and I felt heavy at heart, knowing somewhere out there was a family or loved ones missing this person, wondering what happened to them.

"What can you say about it?" I asked. "Looks like it's female, am I right?"

He nodded. "Yes, you can see the pelvic bone over there, is thin and light and has a wide and round shape inlet, you know to enable childbirth. And then there is the femur. The femur of a male is thicker than that of a female. The femoral head diameter below forty-one and a half millimeters indicates the individual is a female, which it is in this case."

"It's definitely a woman?" I asked to be certain.

He nodded. "I will say, at the time of her death, she was probably around her mid-thirties to early forties."

"Cause of death?"

"Not decided yet, but there are injuries to some of the bones in the abdomen area that are compatible with those from a stabbing. But I need to get her to the lab to determine it with certainty."

I nodded, feeling heavy. "Okay, can you tell me if she had any children?"

He looked inside the pelvis, then showed it to me. "See those shotgun-pellet-sized pockmarks along the inside of the pelvic bone?"

I nodded again.

"They are caused by the tearing of ligaments during childbirth."

"So, the answer is yes?"

"Yes. It can't, however, tell us how many children she has borne. Just that she has given birth."

"Anything else?"

"Well, yes, there's this." He reached down and pulled out a small metal device. "It's a pacemaker. The woman had a heart condition that required a pacemaker."

Chapter 18

THE BRIGHT LIGHT from the big lamps they had put up all over the area lit up the neighborhood and cast long shadows on the walls of the Seven-Eleven building next to it. People were still gathered outside the police blockage when Allyssa drove by. It was past midnight, and she had waited until Joe and the girls were all sound asleep before she snuck out. She was in her PJs but had put on a hoodie on top. She stared at the activity in the area, her hands turning clammy.

Had they really found a body?

She parked on the side of the road, then looked at the many police cars. She couldn't see much and decided to get out and walk closer. A small group of people were gathered by the police tape. They were chatting, some standing on their tippy toes to see better. But the police had the area covered with tents and trucks, so it wasn't possible to see much.

"What's going on?" she asked a woman standing beside her.

"I heard they found a body," the woman answered without looking at her. "Like a skeleton. Old bones."

"Really?" she said, trying not to sound nervous. "This is such a nice neighborhood. We don't usually see police activity like this around here."

"The person has been dead for a while, they say."

"I heard it was like an ancient burial ground they found," an older man beside her said.

"Is it that old?" Allyssa asked, feeling relieved.

"I don't think so," the woman beside her said. "My guess is it's that guy who lives across the street from the empty lot. There's always been something strange about him. And he used to have a lodger, but one day, she suddenly wasn't there anymore. That was a few years back. Remember how we talked about it? I bet you it's her. I bet you he killed her and buried her there, thinking no one would ever find her dead body. Poor girl."

Allyssa nodded, thinking, yeah, it was probably something like that. In fact, it could be lots of things. This was Miami, for crying out loud. Lots of people were murdered and buried. It could be a gang thing. They had a lot of that. Maybe not in their neighborhood, but close by.

Yes, that was probably it.

"I heard it was some kid from that TV show they're recording down here who found it," the woman added. "They were filming some stuff, and then she saw it—the bones and some animal trying to eat them."

"What kid? What TV show?" Allyssa asked.

The woman turned to face her. "What rock have you been living under? They've been all over the news lately, talking about it. The four kids are searching for their mothers and making some reality TV show out of it. It's all humbug if you ask me."

"I'm gonna watch it once it airs," the man next to her said.

"Yeah, me too," the woman said. "I'll probably end up gulping it all down like the rest of them. I mean, you have to see what it's all about, right?"

Allyssa felt sweat spring from the back of her neck and pulled away. She ran across the street to her car and got in, feeling her heart pound so hard that it drowned out everything else.

Except for the voice in her head repeating what the woman had said over and over again, *"The four kids are searching for their mothers."*

The four kids are searching for their mothers.

The four kids are searching for their mothers.

Chapter 19

"THEY COULD AT LEAST HAVE GIVEN us separate rooms."

I growled, annoyed, as we walked into the hotel room the TV show had reserved for us. There were two beds, but I had to admit, I didn't much enjoy having to share the room with my ex.

"It's fine, Eva Rae," Matt said, throwing himself on the bed closest to the bathroom. "All we need to do here is sleep."

"Do you still snore?" I asked.

He sent me a look. "Do you?"

I stuck my tongue out. "Very funny."

"I'm serious here, Eva Rae. When we lived together, you would keep me awake at night."

"I would keep *you* awake? You kept me awake."

He made a face.

"Really?" I asked. "I snore? No one ever told me that before."

"Well, perhaps people have just been trying to be nice to you. I didn't want to tell you when we were together because I didn't want you to feel bad."

"But now, you don't mind making me feel bad?" I asked and

opened my bag. I started to unpack, putting my clothes on hangers and placing them in the closet. It was hard to pack for something like this since we had no idea how long we would be there or what kind of surroundings we would be in.

Matt groaned. "I'm having a beer," he said and went to the minifridge and grabbed a bottle. "You want one?"

I shook my head. "Is there any wine? I could do with a glass of Chardonnay."

He laughed and mocked me, repeating my words like I was so fancy. "…A glass of Chardonnay…." He reached inside, found a mini bottle of white, then threw it at me. "Here."

I caught it in the air. "What the heck, Matt? What if I hadn't seen it?"

"But you did, didn't you?"

"I almost didn't. I was about to bend down and reach inside my bag."

"But you didn't."

I took a deep breath as Matt threw himself on the bed and turned on the TV. It was past midnight, and I was exhausted. I just wanted to drink my wine, then go to bed.

"Do you have to have that thing on?" I asked, annoyed. I found my PJs and was about to start changing, then realized I should probably go to the bathroom and do it. It had been a while since Matt saw me without clothes. Luckily, I had lost some pounds and looked better, so I wasn't that embarrassed.

"I have to have that thing on. That's how I fall asleep," he said, mocking me again. He was acting like a five-year-old.

I wanted to strangle him.

I went to the bathroom, changed, and sipped my wine while removing my makeup. Once I was done, I brushed my teeth and turned off the lights in the bathroom. I walked back into the room, thinking Matt had the TV on a little too loud when I realized the loud voices weren't coming from the TV. As a matter of fact, Matt had turned it off and was listening to the same voices.

TOO PRETTY TO DIE

They were coming from next door.
The suite where they had put the teenagers.

Chapter 20

THEN:

"They got him."

Rob was tearing up as he looked at Janet in the bed. He had run up the stairs so fast that he was out of breath. But he wanted to get the news to her as quickly as possible. It was the first good news since the day she was attacked.

They had kept her in the hospital for almost a week before she was finally allowed to come home to her family. Rob had been by her side each and every day while his mom took care of the children and made sure they got to school and were fed. Rob had been so worried that he didn't dare to leave her. Her injuries were bad, and he especially worried about her mental health. She barely spoke all day and just lay there in her bed, staring at the ceiling. She only smiled when the kids came in, and even then, it was vague. She seemed so deeply hurt by the attack; it was almost like it had changed her personality.

"Did you hear me?" he asked. "They got him. The police arrested your attacker this morning. I just got off the phone with Detective Frank."

She looked at him but didn't react.

"Aren't you happy?" he asked. "This is good news. Now, we can get justice for what he did to you and move on."

She blinked, then looked away. A small sparrow was sitting on the windowsill outside, pecking at something. She watched it closely. Rob felt disappointed. He had thought she would be excited and happy and maybe even start talking again. She had been so depressed since the attack. The doctors said it was expected, but he missed his wife. He missed that she was usually happy and optimistic, always loving and believing in the best in people—the wife that he married.

He sat on the edge of the bed and took her hand in his. He looked at it. It was so skinny, so fragile. It was almost like he couldn't even feel its weight in his hand. She had lost a lot of weight being bedridden for these past few weeks.

"Sweetie?"

She looked at him. He smiled compassionately.

"How about we pray? We haven't done that in a while?"

She took a deep breath. He took that as a yes and held her hand tightly in his. He closed his eyes and began, "Father God, we come to you in this time of need. We love you and pray that you will have mercy on our souls. We pray for healing in this moment, Lord—healing for Janet, both in her body and mind. We also pray that you will help us forgive this man who did this to her. We wish no strife in our lives, and we pray for this man to realize what he has done and repent, that he will come to you, Lord, and ask for forgiveness. You will bring him to justice, Lord. Only you can do it. Please, forgive him for what he has done, for he doesn't know what…."

Janet pulled her hand out of his, and Rob opened his eyes. He realized she was crying and had turned her head away from him.

"Sweetie, you must not let unforgiveness take root in your heart. You taught me this, remember? God is forgiving, and we can be, too, not for that guy's sake but for our own sake. We can't let darkness rule our hearts. Please, Janet. You must forgive him."

Janet didn't say anything. She scoffed, then shook her head.

"Janet, this is so unlike you. You're the one who always tells us to turn the other cheek...."

She sat up for the first time in weeks and grabbed his arm, digging her nails into his skin. Surprised at this, he pulled back slightly. She stared at him, fire in her eyes.

"I don't want to forgive him. I will never be able to. I want him to rot in a prison cell for the rest of his damn life, and I hope they freaking kill him in there."

Chapter 21

"WHAT IS THAT SUPPOSED TO MEAN?"

Mike stood up and approached Kim. She stared at him.

"Just what I said," she said. "Those phones and credit cards weren't the last sign of life. What did you think it meant?"

"Then what is?" he asked, throwing out his arms.

Kim looked at her hands briefly, then back at the others. She took a deep breath. "Okay. Here's the deal. My mom called my dad. Like in the morning. Way early. At like three o'clock."

"What?" Scott said and stood up from the couch.

"What are you saying?" Tara asked, confused. "I don't really understand. She called your dad?"

"Why haven't we heard about this before?" Mike asked.

Kim shrugged. "My dad made me swear never to tell anyone. He said it was the best for everyone. I believed him."

"The best for everyone?" Mike said with a hiss. He was raising his voice now. "How can that be in anyone's best interest?"

"I don't know," Kim said. "But he was my dad, so I listened."

"Oh, my God," Scott said, touching his hair. "You have known for all this time that your mom, Marley, was still alive the next morning when, up until now, we were all led to believe that they disappeared and probably even died that night? How? How could you have kept this from us?"

Scott was raising his voice now too.

Tara found it hard to breathe. She couldn't believe this.

"What did your mom say to him?" she asked.

"She told him not to worry. That's why my dad always believed she was still alive."

"Not to worry?" Mike asked. "Why not? What does that mean?"

"Look, I don't remember the exact words, but she said that she was going on a trip of some sort. Listen, I didn't hear the conversation, okay? I only know what my dad has told me. I've asked him about it many times since then, but he never wanted to talk about it. He truly believed she would come back."

"Then why don't we ask him now?" Scott said.

Kim gave him a look. "Why do you think that we haven't asked him?"

Scott looked oblivious.

"He's dead, remember?" Tara said. "We went to the funeral. Kim lives with her grandmother now."

Scott grimaced. "Oh, yeah. I forgot. Sorry."

"Yeah, well, there you have it," Kim said and got up. "That's all I know."

She turned to walk away when Mike leaped at her. He grabbed her by the shoulder and forced her to turn around. Then, he wrapped his hands around her neck and started to press.

"Why haven't you told us this before? Why? WHY? I can't believe you would keep that from the rest of us! Our moms might have actually been alive all this time, and you didn't even CARE enough to TELL US?"

Mike was screaming at the top of his lungs while the rest of them just stood there, paralyzed, until someone hammered on the door, and Tara ran to open it.

Chapter 22

"WHAT THE HECK is going on in here?"

I stormed past Tara and into the hotel suite. I saw Scott standing in the middle of the living room, yelling something I couldn't make sense of, and then I saw Mike with his hands wrapped around Kim's neck.

Oh, dear God, no!

"Stop! Mike!"

I ran toward him when he didn't react to my scream. Matt came up right behind me and helped me get his hands off Kim's neck. Kim gurgled and coughed. Her face was red, and the veins on her neck were popping out. She coughed again, then moved to the side, leaning on the couch. Mike growled angrily, and Matt had to hold him to keep him from going after her again. Luckily, Matt was very strong since Mike was a big guy and one who had very obviously been working out a lot.

"Stop it," Matt said while holding the boy tightly.

Mike growled angrily again. "Let me go."

I attended to Kim, who was struggling to catch her breath. Tara came over and placed a hand on her back.

"Are you okay?"

Kim managed to nod. She was still struggling to breathe properly, but it was getting better. I tried to calm myself, then looked at Mike. I approached him.

"What the heck were you thinking? You're like three times her size? You want me to arrest you for attempted murder?"

That made him reconsider. His shoulders came down, and he stopped fighting Matt. Then, he shook his head, pale, probably just realizing what he had been doing. Anger had taken away his judgment. I had seen it so often before.

"N-no."

"Good. Don't you ever do that again. You hear me?"

He nodded. I faced Kim again. "I think we might need to take you to the hospital—just in case."

Kim shook her head. "No. It's okay. I'm okay. I just need... a minute."

"Now, why would you do something like that?" I asked Mike.

He looked at his feet. "She just told us something she should have said years ago."

"I couldn't, okay?" she said. "I promised my dad."

"You could have said it after he died," Mike said.

"You think I would betray him like that?" Kim said. "What kind of monster do you think I am?"

"Wait a minute; so what is that big secret she should have told you?" I asked. "That made you react like this?"

"Her mom called her dad at three o'clock in the morning on the night that our mothers disappeared," Tara said.

Kim gave her a look.

"What? The secret's out," she said. "We might as well say it. It could be useful for the investigation. I'm sure your dad would like to help us find them if he could."

Kim backed down.

I looked at her. "This is, in fact, very useful. What did she say?"

"Something about her going on some trip and having to go away for a while," Scott said.

"Is this true?" I asked Kim.

She nodded. "She told my dad not to worry but also not to tell the police anything. My dad always believed she would come home one day—until the day he died from that stupid cancer. And so did I. I guess I still think I will see her again soon. I remember always looking out the window for her, waiting for her to come home, and reacting to every car that drove onto my street. I still think I see her everywhere I go and wonder what she looks like now. Will she even recognize me?"

I sighed and placed a hand on her shoulder. "I hope you will get to see her again. I really do hope so."

I stared at her; then, my eye caught something in the corner of the room beneath the ceiling. I walked closer, then realized it wasn't the only one. They were everywhere.

"What in the name of all that's good and holy…?"

Chapter 23

ALLYSSA COULDN'T SLEEP. She was back in bed next to Joe, who was breathing heavily. Meanwhile, her eyes were wide open. Her heart was pounding in her chest, and she could barely breathe.

What is happening to me?

Finally, after trying to calm herself for two hours, she jolted upright in bed. She walked to her desk and grabbed her laptop while looking briefly at her husband. He didn't react to her movements or the light from the laptop as she opened the lid. She sat back down on the bed and pulled the covers up over her legs again.

Then, she opened Google.

It didn't take her many tries to find exactly what she was looking for. The story of the four teenagers searching for their mothers had apparently been all over the local media in the past few days, yet she hadn't heard of it. Allyssa wasn't big on following the news and all the bad stuff they constantly reported, so over the years, she had stopped watching or even reading that stuff. It only made her sad, and she realized she was happier without it. Plus, she preferred to spend time with her family, especially her children, who always brought her joy.

Now, she was back to reading stuff that made her feel terrible. And this made her feel worse than ever.

She read through the articles, then opened more, and kept going for hours on end, reading through every one, learning about these teenagers and their search for their mothers.

"And they're making a TV show about it?" she mumbled into the room, then shook her head. "I'll be...."

She stared at a picture of the four kids, then scrolled further down in the article, where there were pictures up close of each one. Then, she paused. She stared at their faces, one after the other, then at their names written underneath.

"We just want to know what happened to them. We have spent these past three years wondering about it, and we need closure," the girl named Kim was quoted as saying.

She was so pretty, Allyssa thought. But they all were. They are a good-looking bunch of young people. No wonder they wanted to make a TV show about them.

But what had they actually found by the Seven-Eleven? Allyssa tried Google again. She only found small notes from local news sources, but they said it all. A body had been recovered from that empty lot next to the gas station. It didn't say anything about what the police thought had happened to this person or even who it was —just that they had found a body.

Allyssa leaned back, feeling sweat spring to her upper lip. There was no way she could sleep after this. The whole thing was a little much right now, and it was making her feel nauseous.

She stared at the pictures of the teenagers again, taking them in one at a time, looking at their eyes, then at their names. Two girls and two boys. All had grown up in the same town of Russell Springs, Kentucky.

Allyssa stared at the pictures, then especially at one of them, before she closed the lid to the laptop and stumbled to the bathroom. She barely made it to the toilet before she began retching.

Chapter 24

I KNOCKED on the door hard. I was angry and trying hard to keep it in. Matt was behind me.

"What are you doing?"

The door opened, and Lydia's face appeared. She looked at me from behind her glasses.

"Eva Rae Thomas? What...?"

I stormed past her and into her room. She protested, and I heard Matt try to explain to her that he didn't know what was going on either.

I walked to the desk where her laptop was left on with the lid open. Lydia came toward me.

"Are you kidding me with this?" I asked.

She looked puzzled. "What do you mean?"

"Cameras? Cameras everywhere in their room? Where they sleep?"

She shrugged. "We're making a TV show."

"So, you're saying they're not entitled to any privacy just because it's for a TV show?" I asked, quite stunned.

"They know what they signed up for," she said. "It's literally in the contract that we can record their every move."

"Even when they fight?" I asked.

She nodded. "Absolutely."

"You're telling me you were sitting here, watching Mike attack Kim, and you did... nothing?"

"Yes, I can't interfere with the events."

"Oh, you can't? What if he had killed her?" I asked.

"Of course, if it escalated any further, we would have intervened," Lydia said.

"Any further? How much further could it have gone? The girl wasn't breathing; her face was purple. What more do you want? For him to kill her so you can get good ratings on your show?"

"Of course not."

"He could have killed her if I hadn't come in."

Lydia looked guilty for a second, then shook her head. "But it didn't happen. He didn't kill her, and you did come in."

I scoffed loudly. "You people are unbelievable."

"Hey, at least you will be known as the hero who saved Kim's life," Lydia said as I stormed past her. I was seriously regretting my decision to come there. It wasn't worth it. I slammed the door behind me and rushed to our room. Matt came in right behind me. I was pacing by the window.

"Hey, Eva Rae. Take it easy, okay? She's right. Nothing happened to anyone."

"If I hadn't... and meanwhile, she is just sitting there watching it on her computer? Hoping it will... Ugh, it just makes me so mad!"

He grabbed me by the shoulders. "Eva Rae. They're scumbags. I get it. But we're here to solve this case and help these kids. You're too worked up right now. You need rest. How about we get some sleep and then discuss it in the morning?"

I looked into his eyes and felt my heart calm down. Matt had that effect on me—when he didn't bring his girlfriends to my house, that was—because then it worked the opposite way.

But right now, he was calming me down.

And I needed that.

He pulled me into a hug, and I didn't fight him.

Chapter 25

THEN:

"He got two years?"

Janet stared at Rob. She was still in bed, as she hadn't left it for months. The doctor said she was perfectly fine, at least physically, but she was probably still dealing with the aftershocks of the attack. She was probably depressed and possibly also suffered from anxiety. He also told Rob it was vital that she come back into the world again somehow.

"Take her out of the house as soon as she's ready. Take her to a nice dinner or even just a walk in the park. She needs to see that the world isn't dangerous. Maybe even take her to see a therapist."

Rob hadn't been able to do any of that. Janet refused to talk to anyone or even leave the house. She just wanted to stay in bed, staring out the window or sleeping. And she was sleeping a lot.

It worried him.

"You're kidding me," she added.

He was surprised at her outburst. She hadn't shown much emotion since the incident, but now there was anger in her eyes.

"You're telling me that man attacked me in my own home and completely destroyed my life, and all he got was two years?"

Rob sighed and nodded. "I'm afraid so."

"I can't believe it. Here I am, completely devastated, my life ruined, and he can continue his life like nothing happened after two years. Well, he probably won't even have to do all that, will he? He'll be let out after one for good behavior, and then he'll be ready to go and hurt someone else."

"I... I don't know what to say," Rob said, feeling sad. "I was hoping for more, but... well...."

She shook her head. "This can't be it. This isn't right. It can't end here. It simply can't. How did this happen?"

Her eyes lingered on him. It was like she expected him to have all the answers somehow and make this better. And he wished he could. He really did. He was devastated.

"I don't know, sweetie. They didn't have enough on him. Plus, he made a deal with them, apparently. He had some information on another case they needed, so he got a reduced sentence."

She growled. "This makes me so mad. It's all rotten, isn't it? We're too darn soft on these criminals. How will this country ever function if men like him can get away with whatever they want? Attacking a woman in her own home and barely getting punished for it. What is this country coming to?"

He shrugged. "I don't know. But at least they caught him. I still believe forgiving him is the best way forward for our family. I have prayed with the children; maybe you want to pray with me?"

Janet looked up at him. She shook her head with a scoff.

"Pray?"

"Yes, remember how you used to teach the children to forgive their enemies? Forgive those that hurt us?"

She shook her head again. "There's no time for that."

Then, for the first time in four months, Janet pulled off the covers of the bed and got out. She made the bed nice and neat, then brushed off her hands and looked at her husband. He couldn't help feeling joyful at seeing her on her feet again, even if she was a little wobbly after the long time in bed. But at the same time, he also felt anxious. The look in her eyes worried him.

She approached him, then walked past him, holding onto the wall and the door as she left the bedroom, something he had been waiting so long for, but it now filled him with deep concern.

"Where are you going? Janet?"

"Downstairs," she yelled back at him. "We have work to do."

Chapter 26

"I GOT A POSITIVE ID."

I blinked my eyes, not fully awake. My phone had been turned off on my nightstand, and Tyler Fickle had called me several times before I finally picked it up. I looked at the clock next to the bed. It was eight-thirty. Matt was still in his bed, all tangled up in the sheets. We had half an hour before we were to meet the TV crew down in the lobby for today's recordings. We were cutting it close.

"Say that again? A positive ID? From the body last night?"

"Yes."

"That was fast," I said, sitting in front of my laptop and opening the lid.

"Well, once we got the serial number from the pacemaker, it didn't take long. I contacted the manufacturer early this morning, and they found her name in the records."

"I'll be...," I said, leaning back in the hotel chair.

Matt was groaning from the bed and tossing slightly, probably annoyed that I was making so much noise. He loved to sleep, and nothing could get in the way of that.

"Is it one of the moms?" I asked. I had given him a list of the names of the disappeared mothers, so he could let us know right away.

He cleared his throat. "I'm afraid so."

I almost dropped my jaw. I couldn't believe it. How lucky it was that Tara had been so observant at that exact moment.

And very, very convenient.

"And there is no doubt?"

"Not in my mind, but of course, we will also match the DNA. But two people can't get the same pacemaker with the same serial number, so, no."

"That means we'll have to reopen the case," I said. "I'll call FBI Director Horne as soon as we hang up and have her do that."

"Of course," Tyler said. He sounded tired, but who could blame him? He had probably been working all night. I told him to send me everything he had, then told him to get some rest and hung up.

Matt woke as I put the phone down.

"Why do you look all flustered and red-cheeked?" he asked with a yawn, followed by a stretch of his arms. "Who was that on the phone?"

"Fickle," I said, updating my email to see if I got anything from him.

"The head of forensics?" he asked.

"Yes. They have an ID for the body they found yesterday."

He looked surprised. "That was fast."

"Yeah, and get this, it was one of the moms."

Matt was suddenly very much awake. "It was? Really?"

He wrinkled his forehead and ran a hand through his hair, staring at me with surprise.

"I mean, I know it was a possibility, and we were hoping for it, but still? How lucky is that?"

I sighed and updated my email again. "A little too lucky if you ask me, but I'm not complaining."

"What's next?"

I grabbed my phone and found the number, then pressed call.

"I'm calling Isabella. I need her to open the case for me."

Chapter 27

THE AIR WAS thick with anger and resentment all morning at breakfast at the hotel. No one said a word while they ate or back at the suite afterward while they waited for instructions for the day. Mike and Kim exchanged only angry glances and avoided each other while Tara and Scott tried hard to stay out of it. Mike even ran for the bathroom to occupy it before Kim could make it in there, then stayed there longer than necessary. Meanwhile, Kim hammered on the door and yelled at him to get out.

It was all very unpleasant.

"Can't we just try to pretend like we're getting along?" Scott finally said.

Tara looked toward the corner of the ceiling. "Yeah, remember what the FBI agent told us? They're recording everything."

"If for nothing else than to not look like idiots on camera," Scott said, lowering his voice like he thought that would hide what he said from the cameras. "You know, for the entire nation to laugh at us."

"Scott has a point," Tara said. She had started biting her nails again while they were on this trip. Her dad hated it when she bit her nails and always commented on it. But once she got nervous or was watching TV, she couldn't help herself. Her nails looked awful now because of it.

Her dad hadn't wanted her to come on this trip either. As a matter of fact, all their parents, and, in Kim's case, her grandmother, had advised them against it.

"They're exploiting you," Tara's dad said. "They'll use your sad story to get good ratings; that's all. They don't care about you."

Tara knew he was right. But still, she couldn't turn her back on the opportunity to learn more about what happened to her mother. Tara had been close to her mother, and when the journalist asked her questions that made it seem like her mother might have simply left her, that all the mothers had decided to leave them, Tara got very sad. She couldn't for the life of her imagine her mother leaving her on purpose, knowing how much it would damage her.

Tara never believed that's what happened. But she didn't know how else to explain it.

Except that something terrible did happen instead.

"Just stop it, will you?" Tara said, a little louder than she usually spoke. All the teenagers in the room stared at her. Mike finally came out of the bathroom and stood next to Kim.

Tara felt embarrassed at her outburst. "Sorry. It's just… well, it's frustrating that we can't even get along when we're here to help each other through this. We should be supporting one another instead. Who knows what we might find out? We might need each other."

They all went quiet. Mike looked at Kim, then back at Tara. "Fine, I'll behave as long as I don't have to deal with… her."

Kim looked offended. "Why do you hate me so much anyway?"

Mike shook his head with a scoff. "As if you don't know."

"I don't," Kim said.

He paused. "You don't?"

She shook her head.

"Hm," he said. "You're telling me that you don't know that your mom had an affair with my mom?"

Kim stared at him. They all did.

"I didn't know that," Scott said.

"Neither did I," Tara said.

"What?" Kim exclaimed. "What on earth are you talking about?

"They were like… a thing. A couple. I don't know what to call it. But my dad found out about it right before they left on this trip."

"Found out how?" Kim asked suspiciously. "I don't believe you."

"My dad told me that your dad once called him and said he was certain they were having an affair. He suspected something was going on between them."

Kim raised her eyebrows. "That never happened."

"Yes, it did."

"My mom would never do that. Did he really say that it was her?"

"Yes. They were total lesbos or whatever it's called. But they were hiding it. He begged her to stay home from Miami, but she wanted to take off with her secret lover on this trip."

Kim looked at him, mouth gaping. "I don't believe you."

"Well, suit yourself. It's the truth," Mike said, throwing out his arms.

"Take it back," Kim said with a loud hiss. "I won't have you smear my mother's name. When she comes back, when we find her, I don't want anyone to think this is the truth. My mom isn't some… lesbian. You take it back; you hear me?"

"You really still believe we're going to find them alive, don't you?" Mike said with surprise.

"And so what if I do?"

He narrowed his eyes when looking at her. "You seriously think that this TV crew with that retired FBI lady is going to find your mom, who has been gone for three years?"

Kim bit the inside of her cheek, then snorted. "What's it to you?"

He shook his head and laughed. "You must be kidding me. If they're even alive—and I mean that's a big *if*—then they don't want to be found. There's a reason they left their children behind. They'll do anything for us not to find them, and then you have to ask yourself, what even is the point?"

"What are you even talking about?" Kim asked.

"He's making a valid point," Scott said. "What's the end game here? If we find them alive, then we'll have to face the fact that they don't want to see us. They would have come looking for us if they wanted to, right?"

"We don't know that," Tara said.

"Yeah, we don't know that," Kim repeated. "They could be in some sort of trouble, like... like my mom. Maybe that's why she called. Maybe they've been hiding for some reason. We don't know. Maybe they've been trying to get back to us all this time, and we just haven't realized it."

"Yeah, you stick with that little fantasy," Mike said. "While the rest of us live over here in the real world."

"I live in the real world," Kim said.

"No, you don't. You live in this Instagram and TikTok world where everyone sees only what you choose to show them, and you only see the glossy part of other people's lives. It's not real."

She made a face. "Don't you think I know that?"

"Doesn't seem like it," Mike said. "Not with all the posts you make of yourself and the videos, oh, my God."

"Have you been stalking me on social media?" Kim asked.

Mike froze. "N-no. But you post a lot, like constantly, so it's really hard not to bump into you there. It's hard to avoid those pouting lips you always make." He said the last part while making kissing lips at her, mocking her.

Kim groaned, annoyed. "You're such an idiot."

"We do need to realize that our mothers could also be dead," Tara said after a few seconds of silence. "Which is probably more likely at this point. But don't you at least want to know if they're dead?"

Mike shook his head. "I don't know what I want at this point. I have my doubts, to be honest. I didn't even want to come here, but you two persuaded me."

There was a loud knock on the door, and the producer, Lydia, peeked inside. She pushed her glasses up as she spoke.

"You're all needed downstairs. We have exciting news. But first, you all need to go to make-up, so you can look great for this."

"What's happening?" Kim asked.

"That's a surprise."

"But how will I know how to dress for it if I can't get any details?" she asked, concerned. Her voice was breaking, and Tara could tell she was trying to hide her sadness. Her pride had been hurt by what Mike had told her; that much was painfully obvious.

"Just wear something normal, like something you'd wear hanging out with friends," Lydia said. "Like jeans and a top. You'll be fine.

"But I brought all these dresses?" Kim said. "And I never wear jeans and a top. It's just not enough."

"Or you can wear one of those if that makes you more comfortable," Lydia said, looking at her iPad. "As long as you're all downstairs for make-up in ten minutes. This is going to be a big day."

She closed the door and left the teenagers. They all stared at the door, then at each other.

"What do you think is going on?" Scott asked, addressed to Tara.

She felt her knees go soft as she looked into his deep brown eyes. He was so handsome that it almost hurt. Why did she always feel so nervous around him? She felt like such a cliché.

She shrugged and looked away. "I don't know. But with that look Lydia had in her eyes, it can't be good."

Chapter 28

ALLYSSA HAD the TV running in her bedroom while she folded the children's laundry. She stared at the news anchor as he told the story of the body found in an empty lot behind the Seven-Eleven. Then they cut to a reporter live on the scene who repeated most of what he had already said in the studio but added that the forensic experts had identified the deceased, but it was not yet public who she was.

"They won't tell us until they have alerted the relatives," she ended her report.

Then they cut back to the news anchor in the studio, who let the viewers know that they would keep them updated on this story as it developed throughout the day.

Allyssa felt her heart rate go up as she placed the socks on one side of the bed and the shirts on the other. She kept staring at the screen even long after they started another story about financial negotiations at Miami City Hall. She wasn't listening anymore, but she could still hear the reporter's voice in her mind. The fact that they had made an identification filled her with both anxiety and relief. This could be the end of it.

But it could also be the beginning of something worse.

Allyssa shook the thought and put the socks and folded shirts back in the hamper, then walked to her stepdaughter's room and placed it on the floor so she could put it away when she came home, as was her job. Then she put all the toddler's clothes away. She paused as she looked at the old teddy bear staring at her from Kaylee's bed.

Then, she thought of something.

She hurried to the garage, removed the hatch, and pulled down the ladder leading to the small attic. She crawled up there and went to the back, where she had a couple of boxes of her old stuff—the few things she had. She pulled out an old sweatshirt and a couple of books that Joe had given her when they first met. There, on the bottom, was a small box. She opened it and dug through old memorabilia from the beginning with Joe, and there it was. She pulled it out and looked at it.

The small purple heart glistened even in the sparse light.

And it filled Allyssa with such deep sadness that she burst into tears. With the other hand, she clasped her mouth and held back her sobs. So many memories and emotions overwhelmed her at this moment; she could barely take it.

How life had pulled a trick on her.

Allyssa scoffed, then put the necklace back in the box. She closed the lid and put everything back where it had been. She hadn't looked at that thing in so many years; she had almost forgotten she had it.

Almost.

But not a day passed without her thinking of the person who wore it.

"We're back! We forgot something. Again!"

The voice came from downstairs, and Allyssa gasped lightly. It was Joe and the kids. They had left for school and daycare but must have forgotten something important. Sabrina always did.

Allyssa wiped the tears from her eyes with the back of her hand, then crawled down the ladder and closed the hatch just as her stepdaughter came out to find her.

"Hi, sweetie," she said, her voice breaking.

Sabrina stared at the ceiling and the hatch that was almost closed. "What are you doing?"

"I'm… I was just… looking for something but didn't find it." Her stepdaughter gave her a suspicious look.

"You never go up there? What's up there anyway?"

Allyssa smiled and turned her stepdaughter around by the shoulders. "So… what did you forget this time, huh? I think one of these days, you'll forget your own head."

That made her laugh and forget about the hatch.

"I forgot my lunch," she said and rushed inside, grabbed the lunch, and ran to her dad, who was waiting by the door, looking annoyed that he would be late now too.

Chapter 29

"LISTEN, I don't have all day for this."

I looked at my watch, then up at Lydia. She smiled sheepishly back at me, then chirped.

"It won't be much longer now. We're almost ready for you. Remember, you signed a contract; you can't back out now."

I had been waiting in the lobby for almost two hours, and it was about to drive me nuts. I thought we were supposed to do the take right away, but there kept being things they needed to fix or set up.

"Everything takes forever when it comes to producing television," Lydia said, reading my mind. "It can be a drag. I know."

"Yeah, well, I kind of want to go to the site where the body was found and talk to them there, then head to Miami PD downtown and talk to the detective on the case. Isabella Horne, you know, the director of the FBI, has opened the case of the disappeared mothers and put me in charge of it. I'm kind of anxious to get to work, so could you maybe push them a little in there and tell them to get a move on?"

Matt chuckled next to me, then tried to hide his amusement by covering his mouth with his hand.

"Y-yes, of course," Lydia said and got up from the leather chairs we were sitting in. I was going out of my mind just sitting there when there was a murder case I needed to attend to.

"What are you laughing at?" I said to Matt.

"You," he said.

"Oh, do you find this funny?"

"No, just you. You really can't stand these people, can you?" he said, leaning forward.

I exhaled. "No, you're right. I can't. What the heck are they even doing in there? What is there to set up?"

"Lights, microphones, and the kids need make-up and stuff," Matt said. "Maybe they're even doing a few short interviews with them before they send you in."

I closed my eyes and shook my head. "It's all your fault, you know?"

"My fault? How so?"

"You convinced me to do this."

"You needed the money, so there really wasn't much to argue about," he said. "It will be over before you know it, and then we can focus on solving the case."

"I thought they would be following us around while we did police work, not us sitting here waiting for them to get ready, to get the lights right. I don't care about lights."

"But they do. They want to make everything look great," Matt said and put a hand on my arm.

He was trying to calm me down, and it was working. He was right. I had agreed to do this, so I had to play by their rules. It was, after all, a lot of money we were talking about and the possibility of doing more shows.

If I could last that long.

"Why is it taking forever?" I growled and stood to my feet. I paced back and forth. "Don't they know we have a killer to catch?"

The double doors to the conference room swung open, and

Lydia came out, followed by the journalist and host of the show, Barbara. They smiled widely and looked at me in great anticipation.

"We're ready for you."

Lydia was holding something that she handed to me. It was a black rose. I took it, then looked at her, surprised.

"What's this for?"

"I'll show you. Follow me."

Chapter 30

THEN:

It was exciting to see Janet passionate about something again. She went from not leaving the bed for months to barely sleeping at all in just a few weeks. Rob watched her as she read through the internet, and then looked into big books, and made one call after another. She held meetings at their house once a week, and after a month, the meetings grew so large they could barely fit them all in the Mansion's living room.

People were talking loudly, drinking coffee, and eating the appetizers she put out. Rob made sure everyone was well taken care of, while Janet led the discussion groups and debated with the many people that came.

It was truly spectacular.

Just the way she sat there on the armrest of a chair because they had run out of chairs, with her glasses on the tip of her nose, listening to people tell their stories, nodding along with compassion.

He was falling in love with her all over again.

The only thing he didn't like much was the reason she had all these people gathered—the cause they were fighting for.

Harsher punishment for criminals.

Rob didn't believe in that. He never had. He believed in forgiveness and second chances and that people did things like that because they had no other way out—because they were in need.

And in the past, that had been what Janet believed as well. But not anymore. Now, she wanted to fight for people like her own attacker to get punished harder and not be let out of jail. Heck, she was even advocating for the death penalty and saying she believed it should be used more often.

An eye for an eye. A death for a death.

So now, she had started lobbying. Rob didn't know much about how that worked, but it kept her busy, and sometimes she would even leave for days to go and have meetings with politicians at the state capitol. Her engagement made her group grow fast, and soon she was even featured on television, where she talked about her cause.

Rob watched her go against another woman advocating for more understanding and maybe even looser punishments.

"We need to be fair and give these people a fair chance in life. Most of them never had that," she said.

Then, it was Janet's turn.

"All we want is safety for our communities. And we don't have that with these people on the loose. They need to be punished, or they will do it again. It's actually not that complicated. The man who attacked me already had two priors on his record for home invasions with violence. Why was he not in jail? Why was he free to come attack me in my own home? You're talking about fair here? That's not fair to me or my family, is it?"

Rob listened to them argue, then turned it off with a heavy sigh. Janet came home half an hour later, and he was sitting in the dark.

"Why are you still up?" she asked, turning on the light.

He tried to smile. He loved this woman so much, so deeply, but it was hard for him to recognize her anymore.

"I... I couldn't sleep."

She put down her purse, then walked to him, head tilted. "Are you okay?"

She bent down and kissed him, then looked deeply into his eyes. "I'm sorry. I haven't been much of a mother or housewife these days."

"It's okay. We miss you, though."

She kissed him again with a light chuckle. He wanted to tell her that not only did he miss her physically, but also on every other level. She wasn't the same, and it made him so sad.

She put her jacket on a hanger and put it into a closet. "Can you believe that woman today?" she then said. "She didn't stand a chance against me."

"She made a fair point, though," he said.

She closed the closet and looked at him. "What?"

"A lot of these criminals never had a chance in life. And I did like what she said about restorative justice. You know the story she told where the victim met her husband's killer and forgave him, and at the same time, she received closure because she got answers to all her questions. I really liked that."

Janet paused. She stared at him, then scoffed. "You are into that mumbo jumbo? What the heck? So now, it's okay just to break into someone's home and attack them, maybe even kill them, if we just talk about it afterward? If we just meet each other and sing *Kumbaya*?"

She was gesturing wildly as she spoke.

"No, that's not what I meant...."

"You want me to meet my attacker and forgive him? And then, it's all good? The nightmares I have will be gone? The anxiety I feel whenever someone knocks on our door or even drives by outside will just magically disappear?"

He sighed and shook his head. "That's really not for me to...."

"I can't believe you, Rob. After all I've been through. After all I have mobilized and fought, you tell me this? That you're not even on my side?"

"I don't really think it's about sides. I'm just more... well, I believe they're humans too, I guess."

She scoffed loudly. "Oh, they're humans, are they? Heck, no. The moment he decided to attack me, he became not human anymore. He became a monster, and the justice system was supposed to give me justice but failed. I can't believe you, Rob. I don't even want to look at you right now."

She groaned loudly, then walked up the stairs and slammed the bedroom door. Rob spent that night on the couch and several others after that. He only once asked her if she wanted to move somewhere else—if there were too many bad memories for her there, but she just answered by telling him there was no way she would let *them* win. They weren't going to chase her out of her own home; that was for sure.

Rob never asked her again, and for the sake of their marriage, he never debated her cause with her again, either.

Chapter 31

SHE LOOKED VERY UNCOMFORTABLE. The FBI agent with red hair and chubby cheeks seemed tired of her life as she entered the room where the kids had been waiting. The cameras were rolling, and Tara watched as Kim straightened her back and fixed her long dark hair. She made pouting lips and blinked her artificial eyelashes excessively.

Tara rolled her eyes.

The FBI woman walked in and was greeted by the anchor, Barbara, with open arms. She looked uncomfortable as they hugged.

In her hands, she had a black rose.

Barbara addressed the teenagers. They had them lined up in the middle of the room with high ceilings and marble floors. They had been told the place was usually used for weddings.

"Kids," Barbara said and walked closer. The cameras followed her closely. She tilted her head and paused for effect. "As you all know, a body was discovered yesterday, and now we know the identity of the person you found. I can tell you it was one of your mothers."

She paused for effect again, and Tara felt a rush of fear go through all four of them. She held her breath. What was this? What were they doing?

"I sense that you all went quiet," Barbara said. "What are you feeling right now? Mike?"

Mike's eyes became big. He was searching for the words. Tara felt terrible for him. To be put on the spot like that?

"I... I...."

Barbara nodded compassionately. "Does it scare you?"

"Well, yes, of course," he said. "A part of us has always hoped they would come back, but I think I speak for all of us when I say that we also knew that the possibility of actually seeing them again —alive—was really small."

"Speak for yourself," Kim said and touched her hair. "I know my mom is alive. I will see her again."

"Scott?" Barbara said, turning to face him. "You've been very quiet all day. How do you feel right now?"

"Not good," he said. "But I've come here for closure, and like Mike, I knew it was a big possibility that we would find out they were dead."

"But you still hang onto that hope, right?" Barbara said.

"Right."

She faced Tara. "Tara?"

Tara felt her heart rate go up. Was it her mother they had found? She fought her tears.

"Y-yes?"

"What are you thinking?"

She cleared her throat, feeling how it was closing up. "I... I don't know. Scared, I guess. Terrified."

"That's understandable," Barbara said and looked at the FBI woman with the black rose in her hands.

"Agent Thomas?"

She stepped forward and barely looked at them. "Am I right in saying that this identification was unusually quick?"

Agent Thomas nodded. "Yes. It was done very fast due to the fact that the deceased had a pacemaker. There's a serial number on them, and as soon as we contacted the company behind it, we knew who had that specific pacemaker."

A small whimper came from Kim at the end of the lineup. Barbara saw it and reacted. She took the black rose from the agent and handed it to Kim.

"Kim. Your mother suffered from heart failure and had a pacemaker. The victim was your mother, Marley. I'm very sorry for your loss."

Chapter 32

IT WAS by far the worst thing I had ever been a part of. I felt awful as I watched Kim fall to her knees, overwhelmed by tears and grief. The other teenagers embraced her and tried to comfort her while the cameras were rolling and getting their reactions from all angles.

It made me want to throw up.

I turned around and started to walk out of the room. I pushed the door open and gasped for air as I entered the lobby. I could barely breathe; that's how awful I felt. I had to bend forward and lean my hands on my knees. Matt came up behind me. I felt his hand on my shoulder.

"What happened to you?"

I shook my head. "I can't... did you see that poor girl? Did you see her face as her world fell apart? How can they do that to her and record everything? She's nothing but a child."

"She did sign a contract," Matt said. "She knew what she was getting herself into, and technically, she's an adult."

I looked up at him. "How can you be so cynical? Didn't your heart break for that poor girl in there?"

"Sure, I can't say I wasn't devastated for her," he said. "I felt bad, but…."

"But what?" I stopped him. "What can justify this?"

"She agreed to do this, knowing she might find out her mother was dead. It's just the reality."

I stared at him and then shook my head. "Wow. I can't believe you. I'm gonna leave now and pretend we never had this conversation."

"Where are you going?" Lydia said, coming up behind us almost creepingly. We hadn't heard or seen her, so she scared us as she suddenly spoke.

"We need you for the second part."

"There's a second part? This wasn't enough?" I asked.

She looked at her iPad through her glasses. "Next up is the detail section where you explain to Kim what happened to her mother and how you will try to figure out who killed her."

I stared at her, almost feeling like laughing if it hadn't been so absurd. This whole situation was beyond bizarre.

"I'm not staying for any more," I said. "I need to get to the site and then to the police station to get more details. I don't have time for your little games."

Lydia cleared her throat, then took off her glasses. "I understand you're busy, but I must remind you that we have a contract. If you leave now, you will be in breach of that."

I closed my eyes—that darn contract. I had taken this job for the money, but was it worth it? I wasn't sure anymore.

Lydia smiled or tried to. It came out awkward. "We're ready for you. They're setting up the chairs for your little chat as we speak."

I stared at Matt like I expected him to say something to help me, but he just shrugged, then said, "We did sign a contract. We can do the police work after—when we're done."

I had never in my life put anything before solving a murder case. Was this what I had come to?

I shook my head. "I'm sorry. I have work to do. I have to go."

Part III

TWO DAYS LATER

Chapter 33

IT WAS RAINING HEAVILY, but that didn't stop Nate and his three buddies from doing what they loved. They drove in Nate's pick-up truck to the bridge at the river by the old railroad tracks and parked by the shore underneath it. It was the perfect place for their newest hobby.

Magnet fishing.

They had only been doing it for a few months, but it was always an adventure, and they always found the coolest stuff—mostly wedding rings and other jewelry, but also tons of old guns that were completely crusty from being in the murky water for so long. People would throw all kinds of stuff from the bridge above, thinking it would be lost forever in the brown river water. Often, it was things like shopping carts, motorcycles, and rifles, and once, they even found a safe with coins and jewelry inside.

It was so cool.

They got out of the truck, giggling with anticipation, then they each pulled out their magnets from the back. They were attached to a long rope that they threw in the water, and as soon as it attached itself to something, they'd pull it in.

"I hope I find another gun," Nate said. "Maybe one that the police have been looking for. Oh, like it might be wanted in like a mafia murder case or something cool like that."

He bobbed his head while his friends laughed. They each took their big heavy magnets and tossed them as far as possible into the water.

CLONK

Nate had something right away. The anticipation of what it could be almost killed him. He pulled it in. His three buddies stepped up to see what it was. A round brown metal thing came out of the water. It had green seaweed growing on it and looked rusty.

Nate held it up in the air.

"What the heck is that?"

"Looks like part of the wheel of a car, like the inner part," his friend Bobby said. "But it's hard to tell."

"Cool," Nate said as he put it on the ground, then detached it from the magnet.

Bobby then pulled out something else, and they all went to look at what it was.

"A speedometer," Nate said just as Pete pulled out what looked like the bumper of a car.

"Whoa," Nate exclaimed.

He was getting excited. There was definitely something big down there, and he wanted to see what it was. It had to be a car. He had heard of others who went magnet fishing and pulled out parts of a car and sometimes even an entire car, and he dreamt of doing it too. He had even seen videos of people doing it on YouTube. But he had never thought he might do it himself.

Nate threw out his magnet in the direction where Pete had found the bumper. It attached itself to something immediately, and he tried to pull it, but it was too heavy for him.

"Hey, guys, I'm gonna need some help here," he said, straining to pull it.

The three others also threw in their magnets, and they soon

clung to whatever it was down there. Then, they all pulled. All four of them were big guys, but this was really heavy, and they struggled to move it.

"Take the grappling hook out of the truck," Nate yelled to Bryan. "It might help us."

He let go of his magnet, then ran to get it and came back. The massive thing they had caught had moved closer to the surface. Bryan threw in the hook and attached it to the item on the second try. And then, they all pulled.

Seconds later, the river sighed deeply and revealed the roof of an SUV. The boys pulled it, then let go of it and had to rest to catch their breath.

That beast was heavy.

"Hey, there's something inside it," Bryan said, approaching the front seat, going into the water until he was hip-deep. They all ran to look, but once Nate saw what it was, he turned around and hurried back to the shore. Then, he grabbed his phone and dialed nine-one-one while trying to calm his throbbing heart.

Chapter 34

SHE WAS DOING the dishes while the rain poured down outside. It had been raining for two days in a row now, like a flood, and her yard had become flooded. The children wanted to go outside and play in the puddles, but Allyssa had told them no. Instead, she had put on a movie in the living room and made them popcorn.

She could hear the song *We Don't Talk about Bruno* coming from in there and chuckled as she realized how loudly the children were singing along. They loved that movie, *Encanto*. They had watched it endlessly since it came out and knew all the songs, of course. Even her toddler, Kaylee, except it was only her mother who could actually make out the words that came out of her mouth from behind the binky.

Allyssa shook her head and smiled. She loved the sound of Kaylee's voice. She was definitely going to be the musical one in the family. Sabrina couldn't carry a tune if her life depended on it. She wasn't very creative in general, even though she tried to be. It just came easier to her half-sister. But Sabrina was very strong-willed, so she would definitely get her way in life somehow. There was no doubt about it. And if she didn't have the talent for something, she would work her way to accomplish it. That was her nature.

Allyssa put down the plate, then stared at the door to the living room. Why couldn't she hear Sabrina singing? Even though it sounded terrible, she usually always chimed in when her little sister started singing—sometimes even louder than Kaylee, much to her sister's frustration.

A frown grew between Allyssa's eyes.

She felt a nagging sensation in the pit of her stomach and decided she needed to check on them. There was probably nothing wrong; maybe Sabrina was just in the bathroom, but something told Allyssa that she had to take a look—just to be sure—just in case.

She opened the door to the living room, where music blasted from the TV. Kaylee sat on the couch, bundled under a blanket with the popcorn bowl in her lap. She stopped singing as her mom walked in.

The seat next to her was empty.

"Where's Sabrina?" Allyssa asked. "I thought she was watching the movie with you?"

Kaylee shook her head, then shrugged.

"Ah, okay."

Allyssa smiled, thinking she was just being silly. Sabrina was a big girl, and if she wanted to go to her room and hang out, then, of course, she could do that. She walked back into the kitchen and didn't see her stepdaughter standing there at first. Once she did, she grasped her chest.

"Oh, boy, you scared me."

Sabrina held something in her hands, which she held out to her stepmother. It was a small box. Allyssa could barely breathe as she looked at it.

"Where did you get that?"

"I found it up in the attic."

Allyssa stared at the box, then at the necklace around her step-daughter's neck.

"It had this in it. It's so pretty, don't you think?"

"Please, take it off," Allyssa said, reaching for it.

Sabrina shrieked and pulled back. "No! I love it. I wanna keep it."

"It's not yours," she said a little more angrily than she wanted to. "It's mine. You can't just take my things."

Sabrina burst into tears that soon turned into wailing. Soon, her dad came rushing into the kitchen and looked at them.

"What on earth is going on here?"

"I found this necklace, and now Allyssa wants to take it from me."

Joe looked at Allyssa, a deep frown growing between his eyes. "Why can't she wear it?"

"It's... it's mine," Allyssa said.

"So? You never wear it anyway. I've never seen it before."

"It's so pretty," Sabrina said.

"I... I just don't want her to lose it; that's all. It's special to me," Allyssa said. "You know how she is with things."

Joe scoffed. "That's a little harsh. She's eight years old. You're being a little crazy there, don't you think? What harm can it do if she wears it, huh?"

"I bet she would let Kaylee wear it," Sabrina said.

"What harm does it do, huh?" Joe repeated.

"I... guess... none," she said. She stared down at the pendant on the necklace and touched it gently with an exhale.

"I guess you can wear it, then."

Sabrina squealed with joy. "Yay, thank you so much. I can't wait to show it to my friend, Mia. She's gonna be so jealous."

Sabrina ran out of the kitchen, and Joe came up to Allyssa. "See, you made her very happy. Wasn't that worth it?"

Allyssa sighed again. "I guess so."

"It's an ugly necklace anyway," he said, sorting through the mail on the table. "Where did you get it?"

Allyssa returned to wiping the dishes. She felt a pinch in her stomach and a tear shaping in the corner of her eye.

"I... I don't really remember."

He leaned over and kissed her. "See. It can't be that important to you if you never wear it and don't even remember how you got it."

She nodded and closed her eyes when he kissed her on the forehead. "I think you were just being silly. And now, your stepdaughter loves you, thanks to me."

He left, whistling loudly while Allyssa felt the tear escape her eye and wiped it away with the palm of her hand. Seeing the necklace again made her feel so emotional; she could barely contain herself.

You can't let them know.

She took another deep breath and decided to put it away—back where she had hidden it for the past three years.

No one can ever know.

Chapter 35

I WAS in breach of contract. I knew I was, but at this point, I no longer cared. I felt awful for Kim and wanted to find out what happened to her mom. Initially, that's what I thought the production company wanted me to do, not to play some role in some sick reality show with no regard for the victims and what they went through. I wasn't an actress; for that, they'd have to get my sister.

I was sitting at Miami PD headquarters, going through the files, occasionally looking at my phone as it lit up and Lydia's name appeared. For the fifth time that day, I didn't pick up. She could yell and scream "breach of contract" all she wanted to. I was busy.

I had found something that I believed to be interesting and wanted to follow up on it—a lead if you will. It was a small note in the initial files, but it caught my interest, and I decided to check it out.

"Where are we going?" Matt asked as I got up and grabbed my purse. I looked at him. Did I want him to tag along?

Not really.

As long as we weren't fighting, we were a pretty good team, and

I liked him. But we did argue a lot, and it drained me. I bit the side of my cheek while contemplating what I wanted.

"*I'm* going down to the marina."

I turned around to walk away, but he followed me. "I'll come with you."

I narrowed my eyes while looking at him as he approached me. "Really? You don't have to."

"Hey, I'm here for the same reason as you, to help figure out what happened to those women. To help the kids get closure. Am I sad we're not doing the TV show? Yeah, of course, but that's not my decision."

I walked to the patrol car that Miami PD had let me borrow and opened the door. Then, I paused.

"I just couldn't be a part of it the way it was. And it was stopping me from doing my job. Director Horne told me to take this case, and I don't have time to be part of some silly TV show."

He nodded. "Yeah, I understand. I just hope they won't sue us for breach of contract and all that."

I didn't say anything. I had thought about that, too but decided to push it aside. We would cross that bridge when we got to it. We jumped into the car, and I started the engine, then backed out of the parking garage underneath the building.

"What are we doing?" he asked.

"I told you; we're going to the marina."

"I know that, but why?"

I swung the car onto the road and Miami's heavy traffic, then accelerated.

"There was a small note in the initial reports about a guy who came to the police station after hearing about the disappearance of the four women and said he had seen them at the marina early in the morning hours."

Matt wrinkled his forehead. "Really? And why wasn't that investigated?"

I took a right turn and drove toward the ocean. Many people

going to the beach surrounded me with all their floaties in the windows and beach chairs strapped to the roofs of their cars.

"Because he was some homeless guy, and they didn't believe him."

I took another turn, and we could see the marina in the distance. The huge yachts towered on the horizon, along with massive masts from the big sailboats. These were some of the world's most expensive boats docked down here. Some of them were like floating mansions. They came with chefs and maids and everything you could drink for days—if you had that kind of money, that was. It could easily be fifty thousand to a hundred thousand to charter one for a week. I was never going to be able to do that.

As we parked and walked toward the marina, I couldn't help but feel envious of those who could afford such luxury. The boats were a symbol of excessive wealth, and it made me wonder what it would be like to be able to live like that.

"So, how do you propose we find this guy?" Matt said.

The rain hadn't stopped but slowed down a little, so it wasn't too bad. I put my FBI jacket on, and so did Matt. It could sustain the rain and had a hoodie that we pulled up. I looked at him, then shrugged.

"I didn't say it was going to be easy."

Chapter 36

THEN:

It took ten years before lightning struck again. On a Monday morning in April, Janet was home alone in the mansion. She was drinking her coffee on the back porch, overlooking the yard, thinking she needed to pull up some weeds. The yard was in dire need of some TLC. She had been postponing it and neglecting it for too long.

Janet sighed and sipped her coffee. It was a beautiful day out, not a cloud in the sky, and seventy degrees. And she had the day off. There really was no excuse for her not to get it done. The kids had all left the nest and no longer demanded her constant attention.

"I guess it's just you and me," she said to the garden, then finished her cup and went inside to put it in the dishwasher. She wondered for a second if she should eat something. Yardwork always made her hungry. She reached for a banana, peeled it, and took a bite. She looked out the window at the people walking by on the sidewalk and saw a man on the street.

Why was he just standing there?

Was he watching the house?

Janet felt a chill run down her spine, then took another bite of her banana while observing him. She knew what Rob would say if he heard her now. He would say she was being paranoid as usual. He believed she had been like that ever since the attack. The worst part was that he was right.

Sometimes, she wished she could be more like him—forgiving and easygoing. But it was harder for her. Rob hadn't felt it on his own body. He hadn't experienced the deep feeling of injustice when she realized how easy this guy got off. Janet had always believed in the justice system and fairness, but not anymore.

The guy started to walk away, and she calmed down. She finished the banana and threw the peel in the garbage can. Then, she realized it was full and decided to take it out. She grabbed the bag and closed it, tying a knot, then walked out to the front of the house and down the stairs. She carried the bag to the garbage can and tossed it in. As she closed the lid, she spotted the man again, standing in front of the neighbor's house.

What is he doing? Why is he just standing there? Do I know him from somewhere?

Janet couldn't help herself. She felt anxious at seeing him there. He looked just like the guy who had attacked her. But it couldn't be. Was she seeing things? Was it just a result of her PTSD? For what happened to her? Was she forever going to think that every man on the street was about to attack her? Was that the only way she knew how to live?

I refuse to be that way. I refuse to let them win.

She snorted, then rushed back inside and closed the door behind her. She looked out the window and saw that the man was gone, then laughed at her own silliness. She shook her head, then walked to the kitchen to put in a new garbage bag, just as she heard a bump coming from inside the living room.

Heart throbbing in her chest, she hurried in there just in time to see the man from the street get up on his feet after crawling through her window.

When she saw the gun in his hand, her heart dropped.

Chapter 37

I SPOTTED a man carrying some suitcases. He wore a uniform that told me he worked on one of the boats. I approached him, then showed him my badge. He stopped and let go of the suitcases.

"Can I ask you a question?" I asked.

He nodded. He was tall and lanky, but the way he carried those big expensive suitcases told me he was much stronger than he appeared to be.

"Yes, of course."

He spoke with such politeness; it was obvious he was good at his job of taking care of extremely rich people. He was definitely also British, which made him even more suited.

"I know it might be far-fetched, but we're looking for a man that goes by the name of Mark Benton?"

The man looked at me with confusion. "That doesn't seem to ring a bell."

"He might go by another name. He sort of... used to live around here, I was told. At the marina."

The man's face lit up. "Ah, you mean Pastor Mark. Yes, I know him very well."

"Really?"

"He's harmless. Some people find him annoying, but I'm not one of those. I find his small outbursts quite… charming, if I may say so."

"You certainly may," I said. "Could you also tell me where to find him? Is he still around?"

"He usually hangs out by the park over there," he said and pointed. "The marina has often tried to get rid of him, but since he stays in the public areas, they haven't been able to."

I looked in the direction he pointed but couldn't see anything. It was too far away.

"You can't miss him once you get there. Don't worry," the man said, picking up his suitcases with such elegance that I refused to think there could be anything in them. But knowing rich passengers, I knew there had to be.

"Thank you."

I was surprised at how easy this was going and hurried to where he had pointed, worrying our luck would run out.

It was the entrance to a small park area, and as soon as I exited the dock, I spotted a man I could only assume was Pastor Mark. He was dressed in an American flag top hat and tie, and his face was painted white while he yelled prayers at people walking by, praising God and shouting Hallelujah. In front of him, he had a can where people put money. The guy on the dock had been right. I couldn't miss him.

I waved and approached him. He responded by waving back.

"Praise God; I pray you'll have a wonderful day, my love. Remember, you are His child. He will never leave you nor forsake you. It says in Hebrews…."

I pulled out my badge.

"It's about the four women you saw on the marina three years ago. The ones that disappeared."

That made him stop the act. He cleared his throat and then said in a surprisingly deep voice, "I can't believe it took you this long to come find me. Let's go over here to this bench and talk."

Chapter 38

"WHAT ARE WE DOING HERE?"

Tara looked at Scott, who shrugged. The production crew had asked them all to get into a van and then driven them through town.

"Where are we?"

"This is the yacht club and marina," Lydia said as they exited the minivan and stood in front of her, cameras still rolling.

"And why are we here?" Mike asked.

Kim was next to him, still trying to keep herself composed. The TV crew had followed her every move since she was told that the dead body they found was her mother. Kim had been devastated, and Tara had heard her crying at night at the hotel. She was trying so hard not to show how crushed she was, but they all knew—even Mike, who, for once, had loosened up on her. He was being nice to her, bringing her water when she needed it, or coffee, and even letting her go to the bathroom before him in the morning, knowing very well that she took forever to get ready. Oddly enough, this thing had brought the four of them closer together. Tara had a feeling it was the fact that they all knew it could have been any of them, and they all feared it would be any of them soon.

If one of their moms was dead, they probably all were.

Right?

There was still this small hope inside her—like a tiny glowing flame that refused to die. Tara tried so hard not to give it too much space. She knew it could be crushed in a matter of seconds. And what good would hope do her then? She would only end up being heartbroken, just like Kim. She couldn't let that happen.

"Well," Barbara said, scanning the area like she was searching for something, "Rumor has it that this is where the investigation is going. The police are following some kind of lead to this place, and we've heard they're here now investigating it. Let's go see if we can find out what's happening."

They followed her down to the docks while the cameras filmed them from all angles. Today, they had three cameramen working for them, Billy being the one in charge, telling them what to do. Tara felt nervous at this new development. Who knew what the TV production crew had in store for them next?

Scott was next to her, and he seemed calm as a rock, which made her feel better, at least slightly.

They spotted the Miami Police car parked in the parking lot, and Barbara walked toward it while talking to the cameras.

"As you can see behind me, the FBI is in the area, trying hard to find the murderer. Their latest lead has led them to this marina where some of the world's most expensive boats are docked. Now, what will they find down here? What are they looking for? Let's see if we can find out."

Billy, the cameraman, pointed from behind the lens as he spotted something by the park behind the marina. Barbara saw it, and her face lit up.

"Ah, I see them. It looks like FBI Agent Eva Rae Thomas and her partner, Detective Matt Miller, are in the middle of an interrogation. She signaled for all the kids to look in that same direction and for Billy to film their reactions.

Tara stared at the FBI woman and the person she was talking to, then wrinkled her forehead. She wanted to say something to Scott because it sure looked like they were talking to a homeless person, but then she remembered everything was being recorded, and she didn't want to come off as an idiot on TV. Instead, they exchanged a puzzled glance before Barbara exclaimed, "They must certainly must be onto something important. Let's go see what this is all about!"

Chapter 39

"YOU KNOW, I went to the station three years ago and told them everything, but they didn't believe me. Why are you suddenly interested in this again?"

Pastor Mark stared at us from behind the heavy white makeup.

"We found the body of one of the women," I said.

His eyes grew wide. "Really? Wow."

"We're trying to piece together her final hours."

I showed him a picture of Marley Lamar. He looked at it, then nodded. "Yup, I remember her. She was pretty. Too pretty to die if you ask me. It's so sad that she's dead."

"You saw them up close?" I asked.

He scoffed. "They asked me to sing praises for them. I was asleep in my little tent that I keep behind those bushes over there. There was a guy with them who knew I was in there. He yelled my name and asked me to come pray. He was really drunk and nasty, but I did it anyway. He gave me a hundred dollars. It was worth it. So, I did my thing. I sang and praised God, and they laughed, gave me the money, then took off."

"What time was this, do you know?" I asked.

"It was exactly three o'clock in the morning because the truck that delivers groceries for Publix over there had just passed by us, and it always arrives at three o'clock."

I wrote it down. This was by far later than any other encounters we had heard of. I wondered why the police didn't take his testimony into consideration back then. Just because he lived in a tent?

"Do you know where they went when they left you?"

He nodded toward the marina. "Down there. They walked to the dock and boarded one of the big yachts."

"Did you know which yacht it was?"

"No, but I know who owns it. He was with them...the guy who paid me a hundred dollars. I know him; he owns three of those super yachts."

"Do you know his name?"

"Just his first name; he goes by Malcolm, but everyone knows him down here. I'm sure they can help you find him if he's around."

"And you're sure all four women were with him, and all four went onto the yacht?"

He nodded. "Yeah. Four beautiful women and one ugly old geezer with money enough to spend."

"Did you see the boat come back to the marina again?"

He shook his head. "Never saw it again."

"So, just to be sure, you didn't see any of the women leave the marina?"

"No."

"And you've seen this Malcolm person here since?"

"Many times. I always wave at him, and he waves back. Everyone around here knows Malcolm."

I looked at Matt. "Security footage did show them leaving the club with some man. They could have met him there, and then he asked them to go on the yacht with him and party."

Matt nodded, and I spotted some commotion behind him. I realized Barbara and the TV crew were rushing toward us, along with the four teenagers. It was time to wrap it up.

"How the heck did they know we were here?" I asked, then got up and thanked Mark.

"Agent Thomas, Agent Thomas," Barbara said. I looked around but realized it wouldn't exactly look good if I was recorded while trying to escape. So instead, I tried to smile. I really tried.

"Yes?"

She put a microphone out toward me. "What's going on? Are you following an interesting lead?"

I glared at the woman in the red pants suit in front of me. Her hair was curled the way only hours in a dressing room could make it look. I didn't know what to say, so all I did say was, "Sorry, I can't comment on an ongoing investigation."

"So, it is an investigation; what you're doing right now?"

"You could say that, yes," I said, knowing that wouldn't be giving away too much.

"That man you interrogated right there, he is a witness?" she asked.

I sighed. I knew FBI Director Isabella Horne wanted us to look good. She had the idea that my being on this show would help improve the bureau's image. But the fact was, I didn't care about that at all. I just wanted to catch this killer who had been getting away with murder for three years. I wanted to help poor Kim get closure, and maybe even the other kids as well. They deserved it. No one should go through life wondering what happened to their mother.

"I'm sorry. If you'll excuse me. I have work to do," I said, then turned away and left, walking quickly and determinedly toward our car. I felt like my head was boiling. I was so angry that they had found us.

"Eva Rae Thomas," Matt said, coming up behind me.

I turned around as I reached the car. "What?"

"Why can't you just give them what they want?"

"Because I can't give them anything yet. Once I catch this killer,

I will gladly give them what they want, but right now, they're just in my way. Now, get in, and let's leave."

We got in, and I started up the car.

"Where are we even going?" Matt asked.

I want to find this Malcolm guy before sunset," I said, backing out of the parking lot.

"But I thought Mark said he was here, or at least people knew him here in the marina? Why are we leaving?"

I turned right and made a yellow light just before it turned red. I looked in the rearview mirror but couldn't see anybody.

"I think this Malcolm guy is the key to this investigation," I said. "I mean, we can both agree on that. He's the last person to have seen them alive. But he probably won't want to talk to us. The last thing I want to do is to show up with a TV crew breathing down my neck. We need to lose them."

Chapter 40

THEY WATCHED the news while the children played on the living room floor. Allyssa had recently caved to the rising demands from Sabrina to get her Monster High dolls with a house to match. She had been begging for it for months, and the last time she went to Walmart, it had been on sale, so she had agreed on the condition that her baby sister was allowed to play with her. Now, it was all they both wanted to play with and of course, there were already requests for more dolls and accessories.

Allyssa was tired and had closed her eyes for a few seconds while Joe flipped through the channels and stopped at the local news. She knew she had to get Kaylee to bed soon, but she kept postponing it.

"Five minutes," she had told her about half an hour ago. She was so exhausted from lying awake the night before, worrying about everything that could go wrong. She was terrified if she was being honest.

"Mommy, Mommy, look," her stepdaughter suddenly exclaimed.

Allyssa blinked her eyes. She had been deep into her dream when her daughter had risen to her feet and approached the TV.

She was pointing at the screen. "Look, it's that same necklace. The one I'm wearing." She pulled at the necklace.

"It is the same," she said and looked down at it, then back at her mother, who was still trying to figure out what was happening.

"W-what? What are you talking about?"

Allyssa sat up on the couch. Joe stared at the necklace around Sabrina's neck, then at the screen.

"That woman is also wearing your necklace," Sabrina said.

Allyssa blinked and stared at the screen, where the old picture of a woman was displayed. She struggled to keep calm.

"I don't... I don't think so," Allyssa said.

"It really is the same necklace," Joe said. "And that is the woman they just found down the street behind the Seven-Eleven. They identified her as one of those four women who disappeared three years ago. Do you remember that story? It was huge, all over the news. It even went national. Everyone was talking about it and had their own theories of how these women had just taken off from all their responsibilities, heh. Like they got tired of all the house chores and just decided to keep partying. I guess we were wrong, huh? At least for her."

Allyssa stared at the woman on the screen. She felt like throwing up.

"Why is that dead woman wearing your necklace?" Sabrina asked.

"I guess... it must be a coincidence," she said with an awkward smile.

"That is quite a coincidence that she should be found murdered right around the corner," Joe said, looking at her suspiciously.

Allyssa laughed. "Oh, yeah, hah. I see what you mean. No, those necklaces were very popular back then, some years ago, and I guess she just had the same one."

"But how come you never wear it?" Joe asked.

She shrugged casually. "Oh, you know. They're not quite in style anymore. I never liked it much, so you... hey, anyone up for hot chocolate? I suddenly have a huge craving for hot chocolate with marshmallows. Who's with me?"

Both kids squealed joyfully and threw everything in their hands, then stormed to the kitchen, forgetting all about the necklace and their mother's lies.

Chapter 41

THEY WEREN'T FOLLOWING US. I drove downtown and made a giant loop to ensure they weren't somehow on our tail, but after driving for about an hour, I decided they weren't. They had probably given up on finding us.

I swung the car around and rushed back to the marina. I scanned the area to ensure the TV crew's black minivan was nowhere in sight, then got out. Matt followed.

"What are you thinking?" he asked, looking at me. He was so handsome it was annoying. "You wanna split up and go ask around?"

I nodded. "Yes, that is exactly what I was thinking. According to Pastor Mark, everyone around here knows this Malcolm person. Hopefully, it won't be too hard to find him."

"I'll start over there at the marina's office." He smiled and winked. I watched him walk away and then watched him for a little longer. I realized I had missed this. I had missed us working together and being together. And maybe we were getting better? This was the longest we had been together without fighting in a very long time. Perhaps if we tried again? For Angel's sake?

Easy there, tiger. He has a girlfriend, remember? The one he is texting every ten minutes.

It was true. He did seem very into her and was constantly texting her. I was happy for him; I really was. I wanted him to be happy. He was, after all, the father of my youngest child. There were just days when I wished he could have stayed happy with me.

Focus, Eva Rae. Focus.

I turned around and looked at the big yachts in front of me when Matt returned from the marina's office. He waved at me eagerly.

"They told me which boats he owns," he yelled and approached me. "His name is Malcolm Astor. He should be here, according to the lady there. She said she saw him just a few hours ago when he came into the office. He owns a fleet of boats and charters them out to people willing to pay hundreds of thousands of dollars to be on them for just a few days."

I nodded and looked at the name of the boats that Matt showed me. "Let's go see the nearest one there—*The Sirenka.*"

"After you."

I walked down the dock and toward the ship, then, as I spotted someone on the deck, I lifted my badge.

"FBI, we're looking for Mr. Astor," I yelled to the young man up there.

"He's here, below deck," he said.

"Can we talk to him, please?"

The young man looked confused. "I'll go get him," he said and took off in a flustered hurry.

We waited for a few minutes, looking at this massive boat in front of us. It had to be at least two hundred feet. It probably had gorgeous rooms inside and a hot tub on the top deck. I had always wanted to go on one of those trips on a super yacht, like in that reality show that my oldest daughter watched a lot—and okay, so did I occasionally—called *Below Deck.*

But that was never going to happen with the way my finances

looked right now. I sighed and glanced at my watch. He was certainly taking his time, and it was burning hot to be standing there in the sun.

"Why is it taking so long?" Matt asked. "I'm starving. Can we go get something to eat after this?"

I smiled and nodded when my phone buzzed in my pocket. I pulled it out and realized it was Isabella Horne, the FBI director.

"They're pulling out another body down by the river. I just heard about it. Could be of interest to your case. Are you on it?"

Chapter 42

THEN:

"Please. I don't have much. See for yourself. Take what you want."

Janet could barely breathe. It was all coming back to her from the last time she was attacked—the man in the door pushing and shoving her. The pain, the struggle to stay alive. The fear that wouldn't leave her for months afterward. Panic, anxiety. All of it came back to her and rushed through her small body.

She gasped for air.

All she could see was the gun. It was clutched in his hand, fingers already resting on the trigger. Ready to kill.

"Please... just don't hurt me."

The man stood like he was frozen. He seemed out of sorts. Was he high? Probably. There were lots of drug addicts where they lived, and Janet often saw them dealing in the streets. They had tried to bring it up with the police, but it still got worse and worse. This wasn't the same neighborhood she had moved into many years ago.

She knew she had to be even more careful if he was high. There was no telling what he might do. There was no reasoning with him. All they wanted was money.

"I have cash," she said. "I can give you that, and then you leave, okay?"

That seemed to get his attention. The big man came closer. "Where? Where's the money?"

"I... I-In the drawer by the front door," she said, staring at the gun pointed at her. She had never looked down the barrel of one before, but it was everything they said. Terrifying. Just one little mishap, and you'd be gone—wiped off the face of this forsaken earth.

"Get it," he grumbled. "Now!"

"O-Okay," she said, then stepped back toward the hallway, stumbling over the doorstep.

He followed her. She turned around to walk toward the front door. She could barely hear anything over the sound of her own heartbeat. She tried to breathe to calm herself. Carefully, she took a couple of steps toward the small table next to the door. He was right behind her; she could hear him breathing heavily. His shoes made a squeaking noise when he walked.

"I-It's right over here," Janet said, breathless. She felt all the fears rise inside her, but there was also something else—another strong emotion she'd had inside her since her last attack.

Anger.

It was becoming stronger and stronger as she approached the front door and spotted the baseball bat she had recently placed there by the door in case she was attacked again.

"I'm just gonna get it out from the drawer."

"Just get the money," he said. "Fast."

She reached out her hand toward the drawer, but in a fraction of a second, she continued past the handle and grabbed the bat instead. She spun around and swung the bat at the man behind her, slamming it into his chest so hard that he fell back and dropped the gun to the floor.

Chapter 43

IF I WASN'T on it already, I became on it very quickly. We decided to let Malcolm Astor be and drove up the river to the scene where the new body had been found. I got out and spotted Fickle, then went straight for him.

"I was wondering when you'd show up," he said with a tired smile.

"Tell me what you have."

"Come see for yourself."

I followed him toward the body. It was lying on the wet soil next to the river. An old burned-out black SUV had been pulled out of the water next to it.

The car was tinged with rust, its exterior a dull red, its windows blank and opaque, and its steel frame rusted through. It looked like it was a century-old antique. It wasn't. I looked inside of it. The car was musty and damp and smelled of mold and river water. I gagged a little. The smell was thick, as if something was rotting inside of it.

"The car was submerged in the river, and we had to use a crane to pull it out,"

Fickle said. "We found the body inside of it."

I tried to keep my emotions in check as I approached the body. I had seen my fair share of murders in my line of work, but it never got any easier.

I nodded, taking note of the information. "What about the car? Any leads on who it belongs to?"

Fickle shook his head. "Nope, the plates were removed. We're running the VIN, but so far, no luck."

"The body was in the car?" I asked.

He nodded. "A couple of fishermen caught it with those magnets that are the newest trend and pulled it to the surface, then called for help when they saw the body. It was sitting in the front seat...."

"It?"

"We haven't determined the sex yet."

"How old?"

He cleared his throat. "Thirty to forty years old, something in that range."

I swallowed. "How did this person die? Do we know?"

"Big parts of the body have been burned, so they were in a fire of some sort."

"The car is burned out, so that makes sense," I said.

Fickle looked pensive for a second, then continued. "Yeah, well...."

"There's something that is concerning you, isn't there?"

"Well, I hadn't gotten around to telling you this yet since I haven't finished my autopsy report of Marley Lamar, but there are certain similarities."

"Like?"

"Both have been dead for a long time."

His eyes were searching mine.

"How long?" I asked.

He took a deep breath and bit his lip. "At least two and a half, maybe three years, I'd say."

"Okay."

He shuffled his feet and looked down.

"It's just...."

He was trying to keep his voice steady.

"What?"

The moment hung between us like the air before a storm.

"Well...," he paused and looked a little lost. It was rare to see him puzzled like this.

"Tell me what you're thinking."

"Okay, so both have been stabbed. I see the same type of fractures to the bones in the same area, telling me they were stabbed in the abdomen with some sort of weapon."

"A knife?"

"Most likely, yes."

"Okay, so it is obvious that it might be the same killer."

"But why were the bodies found so far apart?" he asked. "Why didn't this killer bury both of them? Why place one in water?"

I shrugged. "He's clever?"

"It's more than that...."

I exhaled. "The first body wasn't buried there originally, was she? I thought about it when I saw the scene. The dirt was so fresh."

He nodded. "Exactly. Her body looks a lot like this one, and I'm almost one hundred percent sure she has been in the water with how well the bones are preserved."

I wrinkled my forehead. "In water?"

"Yes, I see signs of burns on the bones of both of them too. They were most definitely in a fire. But they were also stabbed and then preserved in water."

"Like the river?"

He shook his head. "No, salt water. A body submerged in salt water decomposes way slower than in fresh water."

Chapter 44

"WHAT ARE WE DOING NOW? Why are we stopping here?"

Tara looked out the window of the minivan. The whole scene at the marina had been embarrassing, ridiculous even. It was obvious the FBI didn't want them there, nor did they want to answer any questions. Still, Tara was getting more and more scared about what was going to come next. They were all getting a little antsy, and Kim and Mike were getting on Tara's nerves. They were suddenly inseparable besties, and Mike was taking such good care of Kim. It seemed odd. Was it just because she lost her mother? Or was there more to it?

The worst part was that Scott had started to show an interest in Kim as well. That part had Tara aggravated. She was the one who liked Scott and hoped he would finally see her for what she was. But now, Scott was sitting next to Kim in the minivan and making her laugh.

Why wasn't he trying to make Tara laugh?

Tara could see a lot of blinking lights outside the van, and her heart quickly sank. What now?

Barbara stuck her head inside the van's sliding door. She was smiling like she was carrying a big secret she couldn't wait to reveal. Billy, the cameraman, and one of his young apprentices opened the back and crawled inside the van. They were filming them as she spoke.

"Okay, kids. Listen to me. There has been another body found. Now, so far, we don't know if this has anything to do with the disappearance of your mothers, but I say we go and take a closer look."

Tara held her breath. Another body? What did that mean? And they didn't even know who it was? This was Miami; it could be anyone—some mafioso or drug lord.

Mike helped Kim get out of the van, and Scott was about to follow, trying to catch up to them, when Tara grabbed his shoulder.

"You don't find this a little strange? Why would they bring us here if they don't even know whose body it is?"

Scott shrugged. "Don't be so suspicious, Tara. This is television; anything can happen. Let's just go with the flow."

She made a face. *Let's just go with the flow? Anything can happen?* Of course, those were the terms they agreed to when signing the contract, but still? What if that body was actually one of their mothers? Did they really want to be here?

She paused as she came out of the sliding doors. The three others had already begun moving toward the blocked-off area, cameras rolling, filming their every move. Tara felt sad and not at all ready for this. Didn't the others realize that this could potentially be traumatic for at least one of them if not all?

Scott put his arm around Kim's neck, and Tara felt jealous all the way to her fingertips. She decided to leave all doubts and fears behind, then ran to catch up with the others. She grabbed Scott's other hand in hers as she reached them and took a deep breath, preparing herself for what was about to happen—for what she was about to see.

Please, just don't let it be my mother. Please.

Part IV

Chapter 45

"EXCUSE ME?"

The woman in the Walmart shirt and nametag stopped and looked at Allyssa. "Yes? Can I help you?"

"I saw that there was a sale on Frosted Flakes, but I can't seem to find them in the cereal aisle?"

"I'm sorry," she said with a sad smile. "They sold out within the first couple of hours. I'm afraid we won't get a new shipment until tomorrow."

"Oh, that's annoying. I could really use them. My kids go through several boxes of those things a week."

Allyssa looked down at Sabrina next to her, then tousled her hair.

"I'm sorry," the Walmart lady said with a shrug. "We're completely out."

"That's okay," Allyssa said, pushing her cart away and back toward the cereal aisle. They would just have to eat something else this week. She knew it wouldn't make her popular, but she didn't have time to get them somewhere else.

Allyssa grabbed a box of Special K. Sabrina wrinkled her nose. "Yuck. I hate those. They're so gross."

"That may be, but it's better for you than those sugary ones," Allyssa said. "You and your sister need to start eating a little healthier."

"Why?"

Allyssa looked at her stepdaughter. She realized she needed to be careful now. Sabrina would soon be reaching an age where she started puberty, and with it would come the possibility of developing an eating disorder. She remembered only too well how she felt about her own body. The self-hatred wasn't anything she wanted to impose on her stepdaughter or Kaylee. Yes, she wanted them to eat healthily; what mother didn't? But for the right reason—to be healthy, not skinny.

"I just want you to be strong and healthy," she said, thinking that was a decent response, at least one that didn't tell her stepdaughter that she needed to start hating her body.

Boy, she wasn't looking forward to those upcoming teenage years. But they were coming, whether she wanted them to or not. Sabrina was going to be a handful. She already knew that. And her mother had left her when she was just a baby, so Allyssa was the only mother she knew.

For a second, her thoughts wandered, and she thought of her firstborn child. Eighteen years old. That was an adult. They could vote now and drive a car. She had seen the pictures online of the kids from various newspapers writing about them being there, searching for their moms. She wondered for a second if she could find them; she would never approach them, but just to take a peek.

It wasn't a good idea.

"What an adorable necklace."

Allyssa was pulled out of her daydreaming by a man's voice behind her. She turned on her heel fast with a small gasp and saw a man bending down in front of Sabrina, touching the necklace.

Allyssa could barely breathe.

"And such a pretty girl who is wearing it," the man said and looked at Allyssa. As their eyes met, she felt the cold run down her spine. She rushed to her stepdaughter, grabbed her hand, and pulled her away from the man.

"We were just leaving. Come, sweetie."

She left the cart in the aisle and pulled a crying Sabrina out into the parking lot.

"Wait, wait, you're hurting me. Why did we have to leave so fast?"

She opened the side door to her minivan and shoved her stepdaughter in. "Just get in the car. Now."

Chapter 46

"SO, you're telling me there is no way this body has been submerged in the river for three years?" I asked.

"I know the difference and can spot it right away," Fickle said. "These bones have been in salt water, not fresh river water."

I stared at the small man with the heavy glasses. He pointed at the areas where it was apparently visible that it had been salt water and started talking about microbes and the differences between being in one type of water to the other, but I wasn't really listening anymore. A million thoughts rushed through my mind as I wondered what to make of this news.

The bodies had been moved; that much was clear. But why?

My train of thought was interrupted by loud voices, and I turned to look at where the commotion was coming from. I spotted Barbara and her camera crew as they pushed their way through the crowd, followed by the four teenagers. They stopped at the police tape. Barbara waved.

"Agent Thomas!"

You've got to be kidding me.

"Hello! Agent Thomas?"

I found Matt and pointed toward them. "What are they doing here?"

He shrugged. "It's a public area; they're allowed to be there."

"No, that's not what I meant. How the heck did they know we were here?"

He shrugged again. "Maybe they have a police scanner?"

"Oh, that's it. You're right."

I exhaled, then walked to them. Barbara smiled widely while the camera recorded everything.

"Hi, there, Agent Thomas. Can you tell us what is going on over there?"

I shook my head. "I'm afraid I can't. This is an investigation site."

"We heard they found a body?" she continued.

"Where? Where did you hear that?" I asked, getting increasingly annoyed with this woman.

"Is there a body?"

"I can't comment on that."

She went quiet for a minute. "Is it another of the four missing women?"

The crowd grew silent around her. I felt like strangling her.

"We have no way of knowing that. Now, if you will please step back and stop filming."

"So, there is a body," she said. "And it could be one of the missing women?"

I shook my head and held up a hand to remove the camera from my face. "Please, just let us do our work."

I turned to walk away when Fickle called my name. Barbara kept yelling behind me.

"But you're not denying it could be one of the four missing women. Does that mean that you know more than you're saying?"

I approached Fickle, tuning her out and ignoring her incessant yelling. Fickle signaled for me to come closer. I knelt next to the skeleton remains on the ground. Fickle pointed at a piece of metal.

"This one had a hip replacement done. Titanium. Do you recall anyone in your casefiles who had that?"

My shoulders came down, and my heart sank. "As a matter of fact, I do. One of the four women had hip surgery a few years after giving birth."

"I believe we have DNA on all four of them in the system," he said.

"The families all provided hair samples back then to help the investigation," I said. "And all their health records."

"Then it shouldn't take us long to get a positive ID if it is, in fact, one of them."

I glanced back at the TV crew and the teenagers. Their faces were all torn in anxiety and fear. I stared at Scott, who had wrapped his arms around Kim, holding her head close to his chest for comfort.

Chapter 47

Rob had a whole thing planned. It was their anniversary, and he had planned to go home for lunch and stay home the rest of the day. It was Friday, and they could sleep in tomorrow. The kids had left the nest, and even the youngest was in college now. It was just them. They would spend time together as a couple for once and maybe rekindle some of the feelings they used to have for one another. Hopefully. He had even stopped on the way and gotten them sandwiches from that small place on the corner downtown that had the good cheese, just like he used to when they were younger.

They needed this.

Work had been crazy busy lately, and he felt he had neglected his family, especially his wife. It wasn't on purpose or even his intention; it had just happened. Life had been so busy for them both. With her foundation and lobbying for harsher punishments for criminals, Janet had come very far. Recently, they managed to get a bill passed that allowed for harsher penalties for premeditated murder and deadly force against an unarmed victim. It was a great victory for them, and Rob wanted to show her how proud he was of her, so he stopped at a flower shop on the way home and bought her a big bouquet of her favorite white lilies. With them in his hand, he got out of the car after parking it in the driveway of the Mansion. Whistling and feeling pretty good about himself, he walked up to the front door and was about to walk in.

That's when he heard it.

It was the sound of something pounding, followed by deep groaning. And it was coming from right behind the door.

What on earth is going on?

Fear paralyzed him for a second as it rushed through his body. Memories of Janet being attacked in the house flooded his thoughts, and panic erupted. He dropped the flowers and the bag with the sandwiches to the ground.

Oh, dear God! Not again!

He finally managed to react and push the door open.

"Janet?"

The first thing he saw was the blood—splattered all over the beige tiles, sprayed on the walls. The table next to the door had tipped over, and the vase with the fake flowers that Janet loved so much had fallen and scattered on the floor. His heart dropped at the sight of the blood, and he struggled to breathe as the panic over-powered him.

What had happened? Where was his wife?

"JANET?"

He screamed her name, and that's when he saw her standing in the middle of the hall. She had blood splattered on her face and clothes, and his first thought was that she was hurt until he realized she was holding a baseball bat in her hands, letting it fall on top of something—some lifeless mass—again and again.

"Janet?"

She didn't stop. Rob stormed to her as she let yet another blow fall on what was below her—what Rob, only too late, realized was the body of a man.

"Stop," he said, "Janet, stop."

But she didn't. The blows fell again and again with grunts from her lips as she kept going like she wasn't able to stop. He panicked and grabbed her, then pulled her aside. Finally, she realized he was there and lowered the bat, panting heavily. Her eyes were like they were in a trance.

"R-Rob?"

Breathing heavily, Rob tried to find the throat of the mutilated man, frantically searching for a pulse while his fingers became bloody.

But it wasn't there. The man's jaw was shattered and his skull cracked open.

"He... he's dead," Rob said and watched as his wife fell onto the bloody floor on her knees, sobbing. Rob looked at the blood on his own hands, then back at her.

"Dear God, Janet, what have you done?"

Chapter 48

"THE CHILDREN DESERVE TO KNOW."

I was walking past the camera crew to get to my car. I really didn't want to face them and tried to walk another way, but they caught up with me. Barbara was yelling at me.

"They need to know if it is one of their mothers."

I paused. I turned and looked at the four teenagers, all staring back at me in fear and anticipation, as if I somehow held the key to everything.

In some ways, I did, but I wasn't allowed to use the key—not until we were completely certain.

"So?" Barbra continued. "Is it?"

I exhaled. "There's no way I can say that yet. We have to wait for the DNA results to come back in order to know."

"But you suspect it might be one of them?"

I shook my head. "I really can't tell you that."

I turned around and pushed through the crowd that had gathered, primarily because of the finding of a dead body but just as much because people wanted to see what the TV crew was doing there.

It was all a little much—a charade, you might say—a circus.

I found the car and got in, then closed the door and sat for a few seconds, gathering my thoughts and hiding my face between my hands. Then, there was a light knock on my window. I looked up and saw Lydia standing outside with her annoying iPad in her hand.

"Yes?"

"I need to remind you that you're on a contract," she said. "You can't keep brushing us off when we ask for details. That's what we're paying you to give us. I know you're busy with the investigation, but you agreed to let us follow you and get the information along the way. It said so in the contract."

I stared at her. I wanted to grab the iPad from her hands and slap her face with it. This wasn't what I needed right now. The way it looked, I was about to tell yet another of those kids that their mother was dead. I knew they all somehow hoped that their mothers had just taken off and that they would find them alive. Of course, they did—anyone would. And I was about to shut out that light and hope inside of them one after another.

It was unbearable.

I scoffed and shook my head, then started the engine. "You know what? Sue me. I don't care."

I backed up the car, almost running over Lydia's feet, swung it around, and stood on the accelerator. I drove up to Matt and rolled down the window.

"Get in. We're leaving."

He stood by the police blockage, looking down at his phone while texting.

"Matt?" I yelled and whistled.

He finally looked up, and I signaled for him to hurry. He got in and put the seatbelt on. I growled angrily at him, then accelerated the car out of the parking lot.

"Do you think maybe you can stop texting your girlfriend for five minutes while we talk?"

Chapter 49

THEY KNOW WHO I AM. *They know where I am.*

Allyssa was sitting at the dining table with her family. Sabrina and Joe were engaged in a conversation she wasn't listening to. All she could see was that necklace around Sabrina's neck, with its purple pendant dangling as she moved her head.

Allyssa grabbed her glass of wine and tried to drink, but her hands shook heavily, and Joe noticed. He stopped his conversation with his daughter and looked at her.

"Honey, are you okay? You're very pale?"

She forced a smile and lifted her eyebrows. "Yes, yes, I'm fine. Just a little tired—that's all. Don't worry."

Try terrified to death.

Allyssa took a deep breath and fed her daughter some pasta from the plate in front of her in the high chair. Kaylee smiled and ate, jiggling her legs in happiness. Looking at her helped calm Allyssa down. It always did. Yet she couldn't stop seeing that man and the way he looked at her in Walmart while touching the necklace.

How? How did they find her?

You're being silly. It was just a nice man complimenting your stepdaughter, whom he probably thought was your child. He just liked the necklace. He was just being nice or maybe even flirting.

Allyssa sipped her wine without spilling. Her hands were shaking less now as she was calming herself. She swallowed the red wine and hoped it would help, but it didn't. Instead, new thoughts hit her and stirred her up again.

You can't afford to be naïve. He knew about the necklace. Somehow, he knew exactly what it was.

She opened her eyes wide and started breathing heavily. Images of Marley on the deck of that stupid boat rushed through her mind, her blank eyes staring into empty air—the blood gushing from her wound right before she took her last breath. It all came back to her and made her bend forward in pain. She let out a small sob, and Joe stared at her.

"What's happening? Are you okay?"

He got up and walked to her. She sobbed but tried to nod.

"Are you choking?"

Sabrina let out a shriek. Allyssa shook her head. "No," she managed to get across her lips. But the overwhelming pain of her memories overpowered her again, and she gasped for air.

"Maybe we should get you to bed," Joe said. "I don't think you're okay."

He helped her get up, and she nodded between sobs. Her torso convulsed in pain and terror as he supported her up the stairs to their bedroom. Joe got her into bed, put the covers over her, then kissed her forehead and gently stroked her hair. She was feeling calmer now and closed her eyes.

"What's going on with you lately?" he whispered. "You're scaring me."

She took a deep breath, then looked at him, getting her act together, trying her very best to sound normal.

"I'm sorry, sweetie. I think I'm just a little stressed out with the kids and such. It'll get better."

He kissed her on the lips, and she felt safe for just a few seconds before the fear came rushing back like a trainwreck.

"I'm sorry I haven't been paying more attention to you," he said. "I will be better. I promise."

She smiled and nodded. She closed her eyes, feeling exhausted, and he got up. "I'll leave you to rest. Let me just get your earplugs from the drawer so you won't get disturbed by the kids' noises."

Allyssa realized too late what he was about to do and opened her eyes just as he pulled the drawer open and said, "What... what is *this?*"

Chapter 50

I CLICKED through the case files on my computer screen. Matt sat across from me at the Miami PD station downtown. They had given us a desk, computers, and access to everything we needed—including coffee, which was my saving grace at this point. Matt brought me a cup and placed it in front of me.

"Here, I thought you might need it."

I growled at the computer screen. "This thing keeps freezing up. It's driving me nuts."

Matt smiled and nodded toward my cup. I took it and sipped it. He was right. I did need that.

"Okay," he said. "Now, tell me what you're trying to look at?"

"It's the old case files. We have all the medical records the families provided when they disappeared. You know, in case they had any diseases that might end them up in a hospital bed, unable to say who they were, if they had diabetes or took any medication that we might trace if it got refilled—stuff like that. I've gone through them before and remembered that one of the women had a hip replacement after giving birth to her son. But now, I can't get this stupid thing to open."

"Here, let me try."

Matt leaned over me and grabbed the mouse. I pulled back, lifting my arms. "Be my guest if you think you're better than me."

He paused. "That's not what I meant."

"Then, what did you mean?"

He pulled away resignedly and gave me an annoyed look. "I was just trying to help. Geez. What's with you lately? I barely recognize you. You seem so angry constantly."

That hit me hard. I knew I had been grumpy. I just didn't know why. Everything seemed to annoy me: the entire TV deal, the fact that I had to take it to make the extra money, and my house falling apart. And on top of it, I had received a phone call from Christine's English teacher telling me she would fail her class if she didn't turn in her missing papers. I had called my daughter about it, but she just told me she didn't care. School was stupid anyway, and the teachers even more so.

Matt received a text and grabbed his phone out of his pocket. He texted back, and I rolled my eyes.

"Well, if you weren't texting your little girlfriend all the time, then maybe I would be happier, okay?"

He gave me a look, then shook his head. "You're unbelievable. I try to be nice. I bring you coffee; I support you even though you basically broke every deal we had with the TV crew, and we might get sued over it. And that's how you treat me?"

I ignored him, then clicked the file again, and it popped open. Finally. I sighed and scrolled through it until I reached the point I was looking for. Then, I leaned back with a deep exhale.

"What?" he said.

"I remembered right. It was Janice. Scott's mom."

Matt went quiet. He put down the phone. "What do we do now?"

"Well, we can't really tell him yet since we have to have it confirmed by Fickle and probably wait for the DNA test. But it looks like it is her, which means we have two dead mothers on our hands now."

Matt nodded, his eyes growing serious. "And we know the bodies have been moved recently and that they have been preserved in salt water for a longer period of time; that's why they're in such good shape."

"And the last person to see them was probably Malcolm Astor," I added. "Taking them on his boat."

Matt finished his coffee. "Let's go have that chat with him, then."

Chapter 51

"I JUST CAN'T STAND the fact that they wouldn't tell us anything."

Mike kicked a lamp in the hotel room. It was evening now, and they were done filming for the day. They had ordered room service and eaten in the suite, all very silently, each lost in their own thoughts. Kim had barely spoken a word all day, which was very unusual for her. She was sitting on the couch, staring into blank air, hands folded in her lap. She had barely moved since they got back.

"They can't tell us as long as they're not certain," Tara said. "Imagine if they did, and it turned out they were wrong?"

"Tara makes a good point," Scott said.

Tara smiled at him. He was sitting next to Kim on the couch and had barely looked in her direction all night. But now, he was standing up for her, and it felt nice.

"They could at least tell us what they know," Mike added. "It's so frustrating how the FBI has suddenly just decided not even to cooperate. That woman is a mean one if you ask me. She's not even trying to help us."

"I think she's just trying to do her job," Tara said, sipping her Coke.

"Why are you defending her?" Mike asked.

Tara looked at him, surprised at this sudden attack. "I'm not. I just think we need to realize that...."

"No, you're totally defending her," he continued, interrupting her. "And I don't understand why. We're your friends. You're supposed to be on our side."

"I didn't know there were sides to take," Tara said.

"Kim, you barely ate anything; don't you want more?" Scott interrupted by asking.

Tara stared at him, her heart dropping. Why was he suddenly so into Kim and not Tara? He almost hadn't spoken to her all day.

Kim shook her head. "No, thanks. I'm going to bed."

She rose to her feet and walked to the bedroom. Both boys got up too and looked after her. "Let us know if you need anything," Mike yelled after her, but she had already closed the door.

"I'm worried about her," Scott said and sat back down. "I don't think she's coping very well with all this. I think she thought this was going to be something completely different."

Mike nodded. "Yeah, she probably thought she would end up finding her mom, and they'd have this big tearful reunion like on those shows where they find lost or disappeared people."

"And then she thought that would be her gateway into a future in reality TV," Tara added. "Did any of you guys think we would find our mothers alive?"

Mike shook his head. "Not me."

Tara stared at Scott. His eyes avoided hers.

"Scott?"

He cleared his throat and shook his head. "Nah."

He tried to sound convincing, but she didn't buy it. She also had that annoying hope inside her—that she might find her mother alive. But that hope was dying a little each day they spent there.

"I'm going to bed, too," Scott said, rising to his feet.

"Good night," Tara said, smiling at him.

He didn't smile back.

Barely had he made it to the door to the bedroom that he shared with Mike when the phone in the hotel suite rang.

Chapter 52

HE WAS on his stupid phone throughout our dinner, which greatly annoyed me. Matt and I had gone to the marina but were told Mr. Astor wasn't there. I then asked the young man to give him my card and have him get back to me as soon as possible. Then we went back and ate in the hotel restaurant. We barely spoke a word to one another. He texted, then smiled and giggled, then texted again.

Meanwhile, I had a cheeseburger and a glass of Chardonnay.

"That's a weird combination," he said when it arrived, and I started eating.

"Yeah, well, I'm weird, and this works for me," I said and ate a French fry, then drank my wine.

That made him chuckle. I couldn't believe I had actually caught his attention for once.

"You've always been one of a kind."

"Takes one to know one."

I said that with another smile. Matt and I had known each other since early childhood, so I wasn't afraid of showing him my weird side. He had seen worse from me.

His phone vibrated on the table, and he looked at the display.

Then, he smiled secretively again, and I ordered another glass of wine.

"You really are into this girl, huh?" I said and ate more French fries. "I don't think I have ever seen you this smitten."

I was trying so hard to hide my jealousy behind my smile. I wasn't sure it was working. He knew me too well. And sure enough, his answer came fast, "Jealous much, are we?"

I scoffed, but it was too much and became awkward. We both knew it.

"Never," I said. "Been there, done that."

We both grew silent and ate. His phone vibrated again, and he answered a text. I sipped my wine, wishing he would just put that thing down and pay me some attention.

Why, Eva Rae? You don't want him, remember?

It was true. I didn't. We had a child together, which was more than enough for me. I just had to deal with the fact that he was moving on.

But why am I jealous, then? Why do I want to take that phone and throw it against the wall?

I cleared my throat and continued to eat. He put the phone down and looked at me. "I'm sorry," he said. "I know it's rude."

I nodded. "You can say that again."

"I just didn't think you cared. But I'm glad to see that you do." He said the last part with a wink, and I threw a French fry at him.

"Don't flatter yourself."

That made him laugh. I loved Matt's laughter and missed it. Realizing that made me sad, and I grew silent.

"What?" Matt said. "Why are you looking at me like that?"

"Like what?" I asked, snapping out of it, telling myself I was being ridiculous—stupid even.

But I just couldn't help myself. Seeing him happy with someone else made me sick to my stomach.

"Like that—all gooey and sad."

I wrinkled my nose. "I don't do that."

"Oh, yes, you do. I know that look. A little too well."

I scoffed again. "You're being ridiculous."

He reached out his hand and took mine in his. My heart stopped for a brief moment, and our eyes met. I didn't know what to do.

We were interrupted by the ding of the elevator opening and the four teenagers walking out, then rushing past us toward the conference room.

Chapter 53

THEN:

They panicked. Rob was screaming at Janet, asking her over and over again what to do. *What are we going to do?* Janet was on the floor, sobbing, crying in fear and angst.

For hours, they just sat there on the cold, bloody tiles, staring at the dead body, wondering how on earth this could have happened and what to do next. They were terrified, paralyzed.

Rob kept crawling to the body to feel for a pulse, expecting, praying, hoping to find one but never did. The blood on the floor was deep red and thick. The blood on his hands was sticky and wouldn't go away no matter how much he rubbed his fingers on his shirt, frantically trying to get it off.

"What are we going to do?" he mumbled.

Janet didn't answer. Her sobs had grown quiet, but now and then, a small whimper came from her mouth, startling him.

They sat like that all night. Why? They were in a state of deep shock, they would later argue. Or maybe a part of them wanted to see if he woke up. They simply refused to believe that this had happened—that he was actually dead—that Janet was capable of killing another human being.

They didn't move until the morning came.

"I think…," Janet mumbled as the sun's rays started filling the house through the windows. "We should call the police."

Rob nodded. He knew she was right. He just didn't have the power to push through his frozen state. He had never seen a dead person before now. And especially not one that had been beaten to death and was lying in a pool of blood.

Janet had said the words, but still, neither of them moved. For that, they were in too deep of shock still.

Nothing happened until there was suddenly a knock on the front door, and Rob's mother walked in the way she always did, with just one quick knock and then swinging the door open with a loud chirp.

"Hello-o-o-o."

Rob's mother screamed. Her eyes grew wide and fearful. Her voice was shrill and trembling as she spoke to them, looking from one to the other, unable to fathom what she was actually seeing.

"What on earth… what happened? Who… why…?"

Rob turned his head and stared at his mother, the disbelief in her eyes, the mistrust, the disappointment, and the fear.

"Did you do this, Rob?" she asked.

He didn't answer. All he could see was the blood on his hands that he couldn't rub off.

"I think you need to call the cops," Rob said, looking up at his mother, tears running down his cheeks.

"You need to call the cops. Now."

THEY WERE OBVIOUSLY BICKERING among themselves as they stormed past us in the restaurant. I watched the four teenagers leave the elevator and rush toward the conference room. They didn't even see us sitting there.

"What's going on?" I asked.

Matt turned to look. "They look like they're rushing to something?"

I looked at my watch. "It's ten thirty at night. What are they rushing to?"

He shrugged. "They're teenagers. Who knows?"

Matt sipped his beer. I stared at the young people as they disappeared through the double doors, still bickering, which made me alert. They all seemed out of it.

"Something is going on," I said, tapping my nails on my almost empty wine glass.

"You're just always on the lookout for suspicious activity," he said, finishing his glass. The beer left a small foamy mustache on his upper lip that he wiped off with his hand. "You can't help yourself. It's in your nature. That's why you're so good at what you do. But sometimes it's nothing, Eva Rae. Sometimes, it's just in your pretty little head."

I looked at him, then narrowed my eyes. "Now, you're the one who's acting suspicious."

"Why?"

"My pretty little head? You never talk like that."

"Like what?"

"Condescending toward me."

He made a face. "Since when is calling someone pretty considered to be condescending?"

I got to my feet and looked toward the closed door to the conference room where the teenagers had disappeared.

"When it's paired with the word little," I said, then left.

"Hey, where are you going? We didn't even pay," he argued.

"Put it on our room. I want to see what's going on behind those doors. I have a weird feeling about this."

He scoffed. "Of course you do. You always have some feeling that we absolutely have to act on. Never a dull moment when you're around, huh? Can't we ever just relax and enjoy a meal?"

Matt caught up to me. He was still talking—well, complaining—

but I was no longer listening. I walked up to the door, grabbed the handle, and pushed it ajar. I peeked inside.

The sight on the other side made me drop my jaw.

"What?" Matt asked behind me. "What do you see?"

I couldn't believe my own eyes. Inside, I spotted the entire TV production crew. Three cameras were set up and rolling; Barbara Bowen was in her red suit, holding a microphone, while Lydia was standing behind Billy, the cameraman, hugging her iPad close. I knew a little too well what was going on there as the teenagers were lined up underneath the lamps. Barbara approached them, holding a black rose in her hand.

Chapter 54

"PLEASE, explain to me what this is?"

Joe pulled out the old photo from her drawer. Allyssa jolted upright in bed. She realized she had been looking at the picture and had forgotten to hide it away properly. Sabrina had walked in, and she had just hurried and put it into the drawer so she wouldn't see. She meant to move it later.

But now, it was too late.

Joe stared at the photo in his hands, then turned it so she could see it as if she didn't know exactly what it portrayed. As if she hadn't stared at it repeatedly when she was alone, studying every tiny inch of it, especially who was in it.

"W-what do you mean?"

It was time for damage control. She had to think fast and decide on a tactic. Allyssa went with pretending like it wasn't anything important.

"This photo," he said and walked closer, holding it out for her to see. She narrowed her eyes and pretended to look closely at it like she didn't already know what it was.

She shrugged. "What about it?"

He shook his head and threw out his arm. "What about it? What do you mean, what about it?"

"What I said. Honestly, I don't understand why you're making such a big deal out of it."

She rose from the bed and approached him, reaching out for the photo, wanting to rip it from his hand, but he pulled it away.

"This is that girl," he said and pointed. "This is that woman from the news—the one they found killed down by the Seven-Eleven!"

"So?"

"So? SO?"

He almost screamed at her. Her tactics weren't working, it seemed. He wasn't buying into it.

"Yeah, so? What's the big deal?" she asked.

"The big deal is that this woman was murdered. They said that on the news. She was murdered three years ago and buried right down the street. And you knew her? You knew her very well, judging from this photo?"

"Okay, okay, yes, I knew her. But it was years ago. When I saw that they found her body, I found the old picture."

"But why didn't you tell me you knew her? I don't understand?" he asked, with a deep exhale.

She sat down on the bed. It was time to change tactics. She went for compassion instead.

"I didn't know how to," she said, on the verge of tears. "I was so shocked when I realized she had been murdered and needed to digest it first. And then it was sort of too late. I feel so terrible for her and her family."

"You knew her daughter, too?" he asked.

She shook her head. "No, not really. I knew her when she was little; that's all. I moved away, remember? Then I came here and met you. Best thing that ever happened to me."

"And the necklace?" he asked.

Allyssa swallowed hard. "What about it?"

185

"It's hers, right? That's why you wouldn't let Sabrina wear it?"

She looked at her fingers, then nodded. "Yeah, she gave it to me when I left. It was many years ago. It just reminded me of... her."

He placed a hand on her shoulder and sat next to her on the bed. "Why didn't you just tell me? I would have understood. It makes a whole lot more sense now—your reaction to Sabrina wearing the necklace and all. I get it."

She lifted her glance and met his, then smiled. "I love you, Joe. You're always so good to me."

He placed an arm around her shoulder and pulled her into a hug. Then, he let go again.

"Wait, where did you say you left from, back when you knew her? I thought you said you grew up in Florida. She's from Kentucky?"

Allyssa rose to her feet abruptly. "I think I hear Kaylee crying. I need to go check on her."

With that, Allyssa stormed out of the bedroom and went downstairs, praying that Joe would be satisfied with the answers he had gotten so far and leave it alone.

Chapter 55

"OVER MY DEAD BODY!"

I pushed the door fully open and rushed inside. Just as she was about to approach Scott with the black rose, Barbara stopped in her tracks. Seeing me, Lydia hurried to block my way.

"Miss Thomas, we're in the middle of a recording here. There's no way...."

I walked past her, placing my hand in the air to make her stop talking. I walked to Barbara and stood in front of her. Her wide eyes with the very blue eyeshadow on them stared at me.

"Agent Thomas, what...?"

I grabbed the rose from her hands. "You can't do this. You have no right."

Barbara looked at Lydia, then back at me. "Excuse me? And do you mind telling me why that is?"

The cameras were still rolling, and one of them approached me. I placed a hand on the lens to cover it. I tried to speak with a low voice, but it was hard, considering how agitated I was. I couldn't believe these people and how insane they were behaving.

"Because you can't tell any of these kids that their mother is dead until we have a positive ID and full confirmation."

"I was under the impression that we already had that," Barbara said. She looked at Lydia, who nodded.

"Yes, we do."

"Besides, they're not kids, Agent Thomas. They're adults and very capable of making their own decisions. Remember that they signed a contract and knew what they said yes to."

"But we don't have a positive ID yet," I said.

"The hip replacement speaks for itself," Barbara said.

I stared at her, completely baffled. How on earth did she know about that? I found myself suddenly at a loss for words, and it took a few seconds before I could speak again.

Meanwhile, Scott stepped forward, and we all looked at him.

"Hip replacement? My mom had that done...."

I swallowed hard. I didn't know what to do or say.

"That doesn't mean that it is her that we...."

"It's her, isn't it?" he asked, his voice growing shrill and loud. "You found my mom?"

I shook my head. "No, no, Scott, listen, we don't know anything for certain yet. Just that the body we found had a hip replacement; it could be someone else."

He looked at Barbara. "But it isn't, is it? It's her."

Barbara nodded silently. "My condolences."

"But...no, no, no," I said. "You have to understand that just because she had a hip replacement doesn't mean that...."

Barbara pulled the rose out of my hand and handed it to Scott. Tears were rolling down his cheeks as he accepted it. I wanted to scream. No one was listening to me.

"I'm so sorry, Scott," Barbara said. "I'm so sorry for your loss."

"But it's NOT...."

Matt came up behind me and placed a hand on my shoulder. "There's nothing you can do, Eva Rae," he said. "They're doing this whether you like it or not."

I exhaled, resigned. I knew he was right. No one was listening to reason here, not even the kids. It was all so crazy and surreal. My focus needed to be on solving the case and stopping this murderer. And I knew exactly where to start.

Part V
NEXT DAY

Chapter 56

HE HAD ORDERED an Uber and was waiting for it outside the police station when it started to rain. Dark clouds covered the sky above him, and within seconds, they opened up and poured water down on him so forcefully that he got completely soaked. Lightning struck not far from him and startled him. Matt looked at the app and then spotted a black car, very much like the one that was in the picture of the app.

That has to be the one.

The car drove up toward him and stopped, and he hurried to get into the back, relieved that he was out of the rain.

"Matt?" the driver asked to confirm it was him.

"That's me. Phew, what a storm," he said. "Took me completely by surprise."

"They tend to do that around here," the driver said, then took off into the street.

Matt had asked Eva Rae if they could—please—go back to the hotel and get something to eat, then go to bed. He was exhausted after their long day, but she insisted on staying longer to go through some more old files. Matt had grumbled, annoyed, and that's when she told him just to go back alone, and she'd meet him there. He didn't like leaving her since he loved being with her so much and hoped they could enjoy dinner together again. But she didn't know when to stop, and he knew she would end up working all night. It was who she was—relentless until she caught her guy. He admired her so much for her willpower, but it also annoyed him because that was the very reason he found it so hard to be with her when they were together. When she was on a case, everything and everyone else ceased to exist. She only had eyes for the case and catching the guy.

It became her entire world.

Matt exhaled as he saw the police station disappear out of his window. He bit his lip while thinking about Eva Rae and how much he had enjoyed this time with her. Even though it was stressful, and she had her outbursts, he realized how much he still loved her. Part of him wanted to try again, but he didn't dare tell her. He didn't know if she felt the same. He didn't want to risk getting hurt again. Plus, he was technically seeing someone else, yet he wasn't completely into her, he had to admit. She seemed a little young and naïve for him, and... well... she was no Eva Rae.

He scoffed and watched the rain hitting the window of the SUV. He thought about their time together and how much they had fought, then shook his head. Was it worth it? Should they try again? Give it another chance?

She probably doesn't want to.

It was useless. They had their chance, and they wasted it. They had a child together, and he was eternally grateful for that. Angel was such a beautiful little creature, and, in that sense, they were tied to one another for the rest of their lives. He would have to be satisfied with that. They didn't function as a couple. It was impossible.

"I think you missed the turn there," he said to the driver and pointed. "The hotel is down that street."

And that was when it struck him. This was an SUV. He opened the app and looked at the picture. The one in the app was a black sedan. And now, he received a message from the driver, saying: *I'm here.*

Matt frowned and looked up from his phone just as the SUV stopped at a red light. The driver turned around, pulled out a gun, and pointed it at him.

"I'll take that phone, please."

Chapter 57

IT WAS ALMOST midnight before I got back to the hotel. Matt had caved in around ten o'clock and begged me to go home, but I was on a roll and didn't want to give up. We had four missing women, two of whom had turned up dead so far. Chances were that more bodies would surface as the investigation went on, and I was obsessed with the thought of finding out who killed them, so we could finally give those teenagers some closure. They needed justice, and I believed I could help them get that.

I had gone back to my initial lead, Mr. Malcolm Astor. I went through everything they had on him, which was quite a lot, not surprisingly. He had been suspected of drug trafficking numerous times, and the DEA had raided his boats three times but found nothing. They'd had agents stake out his boats but had never been able to prove anything.

I spoke to the DEA agent in charge of the investigation for a few hours, and he told me a lot about this guy and his habits that might come in handy. He was a man who liked to party and spend money. And he enjoyed women, lots of them. He was known to invite girls on his boat and take them out to sea to party. When I asked the

DEA agent if they ever looked into him as a possible suspect in the disappearance of the four women, he just shrugged and said he didn't know. The hard part was that the detective in charge of the investigation of the missing mothers three years ago had recently been shot and killed in service, so I couldn't speak to him. I couldn't stop wondering about the homeless pastor and why they never listened to what he told them. Why did they never dig deeper down that lead? Just because he was a homeless person? Couldn't he still have seen something?

It made no sense.

I parked the cruiser in the hotel parking lot, then walked to the entrance. The young man at the front desk smiled at me as I entered and walked toward the elevator. I yawned, feeling tired as the doors slid open with that well-known DING sound when the young man yelled my name.

"Agent Thomas?"

I turned and faced him as he walked toward me.

"Yes?"

"I forgot," he said, holding a big yellow envelope toward me. "This came for you."

I stared at the envelope with my name on it, then took it. "Thanks."

He hurried back to the counter, and I walked into the elevator, looking at the envelope to see if it said who it was from. It didn't. It was just my name written with a black marker.

The elevator reached my floor, and I walked out into the hallway toward my room, then slid the key card into the opener and pushed it. I tried to move quietly in case Matt was asleep. I didn't want to wake him. I had been with Matt long enough to know he disliked being woken up. It would leave him grumpy the entire next day because it was so hard for him to fall back asleep.

I closed the door behind me as quietly as possible, then tip-toed inside the room. But much to my surprise, Matt wasn't in his bed.

That's strange.

I decided he could perhaps be in the bathroom since the door was closed, so I put down my purse and bag with my laptop in it. I then kicked off my sneakers and sat on the edge of the bed with a deep sigh. Tomorrow, I was going to have a chat with Malcolm Astor and ask him what happened that night three years ago. I didn't feel fully prepared as I didn't have much to go on, but it was time. I knew he probably wouldn't be very willing to talk to me.

Barely had I leaned back on the pillow before the envelope began to vibrate. I stared at the end of the bed where I had put it, then reached for it. I pulled it open and poured its contents onto the bed. It was a phone, and it was ringing, but not only that.

It was Matt's phone.

Chapter 58

THEN:

Rob hung up the phone feeling heavy. He almost threw it against the wall in anger but restrained himself. This was not the time for anger outbursts. This was a time for keeping cool and collected, not for his own sake but for hers.

He turned to look at Janet, sitting in the kitchen with a cup of steaming herbal tea in front of her. She was looking out the window as she had been a lot lately, lost in her own thoughts.

She hadn't been herself since the incident at the house.

There's no way around it. You have to tell her.

He walked closer and placed a hand on her shoulder, his heart pounding and his stomach churning.

"Honey?"

"Hm?"

She looked up at him and placed a hand on top of his. A faint smile spread across her face.

"Sorry. I was just watching the squirrel up in that tree. It's really spectacular how fast it moves. See—it's got a small nut in its mouth."

He scoffed with a slight smile. It was the first time he had seen her smile since that day. There had been no joy in her life, and now he was about to destroy the little there was. Take it away again.

It was heartbreaking.

"Sweetie," he said and sat down. He took her hand in his. With the other, she sipped her tea. "We need to talk about something."

Her weary eyes glanced at him, then she nodded. "Okay. If you say so."

He swallowed, then looked down at her hand wrapped in his. She had gotten so skinny; the bones were visible in her wrist and arm. Her fingers were scrawny, and you could see all the veins in her hand.

He almost cried but held it back with a loud sniffle. He had to be strong now, for her sake.

"You know I was on the phone just now?" he asked.

She looked at him, puzzled, oblivious. She hadn't been paying any attention to her surroundings for weeks now. The children would call, and she wouldn't even pick up the phone. The potatoes would be boiling over, and she didn't see it until he came running out into the kitchen and stopped it. She had burned a chicken so much it became like black coal and started the fire alarm.

She shook her head.

"That's okay," he said and clapped the top of her hand gently. "But I was. I was on the phone with George. You remember? Our attorney?"

She smiled faintly again. "Oh, yes, George. How is he? How is Martha?"

Rob bobbed his head and looked at their hands again. "They're good; they're fine."

"Well, that's good. And the children?"

"Also fine, sweetie, all grown up, but…."

"That's good. It was an awful affair with the accident they were in."

"That it was, but they're all fine now. It was a long time ago. But, sweetie?"

"Yes?"

He took a deep breath. He had to say it; he had to tell her at some point.

Just do it. Just get it out.

He cleared his throat and sat up straight in the uncomfortable kitchen chairs that reminded him of school, but Janet loved so dearly.

"They're... George spoke to the prosecutor, and... they're... they are charging you with murder."

Chapter 59

"H-HELLO?"

It was hard to hear my own voice on the phone over the sound of my beating heart. I was scared—really scared at this point. Where was Matt? Had something happened to him? Something bad?

"Who is this?"

I could hear breathing on the other end, making my anxiety go through the roof. Who was this, and why weren't they saying anything?

"Hello?"

I tried again, feeling fear creep up my spine like a cold wind.

"Is anyone there? Hello?"

The breathing became heavier, and a voice said, "Go to room 327 if you want to see him again—alive."

A frown grew between my eyes. I didn't understand. What was this? "What do you mean? Room 327? Where?"

"Do your job; if you're so good at it, you'll find out."

"But what about Matt? Is he okay? Hello? HELLO?"

The person had hung up. I stared at the cell phone in my hand that I had watched Matt use so many times—his black steel cover with the skull on the back. I had always found it so childish, but now it made me sad. I tried to call back, but the person had called from a No Caller ID.

Of course. It wasn't going to be that easy.

I went through his phone and opened all the text messages to see if there was anything in there that could tell me where he was or who he was with, and that's when I saw it. I thought Matt had been texting his girlfriend all this time, but it wasn't her. He had been texting Barbara Bowen, the journalist, letting her know where we were with the investigation. That's how they knew where we were all the time. That's how they knew it was Scott's mom we had found, even though it wasn't confirmed. He had told them about the hip replacement.

"You betrayed me, Matt!"

I couldn't believe he would do that to me. It made me furious, but the feeling was quickly replaced by deep concern for him. Where was he? Was he okay?

Room 327

I grabbed my purse, hurried out of the room, and slammed the door behind me. I knocked on the camera crew's door, and Billy opened it. He stared at me, looking tired but surprised.

"Agent Thomas?"

"Grab your camera and come with me."

His eyes grew large, and he ran a hand through his hair to flatten the curls. "Of course. Give me one sec."

He literally came out one second later, wearing jeans and a white T-shirt, his camera in hand.

"Where are we going? What's going on? I thought you didn't want to work with us?"

"I don't, to be honest. But I'm gonna need documentation, and you will want this for your show. It's a win-win, the way I see it. Now, let's go before I regret it."

Chapter 60

HE DIDN'T REMEMBER what had happened when he woke up. The first thing he noticed was the splitting headache, and then it came back to him. The rainstorm, the black Uber, and the driver and the gun. He remembered handing over his phone and then the gun slamming into his face so hard he passed out.

That was all Matt could recall. Now, he was trying to open his eyes but couldn't move his eyelids. Duct tape had been wrapped around his head, making it impossible for him to open them. His hands were tied behind his back, and his legs were tied together as well. He was lying down somewhere in a small compartment and banged his head against some sort of roof when he tried to move.

Where am I?

Am I moving?

He laid still to be sure. Yes, he was definitely moving. He had to be in a car—maybe in the back of a truck or in a trunk. He could hear a voice. It wasn't far away, so he guessed it had to be the driver. He recognized the voice inside the SUV that he had thought was his Uber. It was his female kidnapper who had pointed the gun at his face before knocking him out.

But why?

What does she want from me?

He tried to scream for help, but his mouth was covered with more duct tape, and a cloth of some sort had been stuffed into his mouth, so he couldn't move his tongue or lips. It tasted awful.

Where is she taking me?

He felt panic sneak up on him—spreading inside of him like wildfire, going faster and faster the more he let it. He struggled to breathe properly in the warm compartment since he could only use his nostrils. It felt like he couldn't get enough air through them fast enough to put out the fire raging inside him.

Will I ever see my children again? Little baby Angel? Or Elijah? Will I ever see Eva Rae again?

He felt like crying. He realized he had wasted all this time. He regretted it so much. Why didn't he just tell Eva Rae how he really felt? That, of course, he wanted to be with her—that he had wanted to since the first day he met her in preschool. That he had known from the second he laid eyes on her, even though they were only four years old. That it had always been them—always been her. There could be no one else. He knew it. She knew it. Who were they kidding?

They were soul mates if such a thing ever existed, and he believed it did. He knew she didn't, but that didn't matter. Deep down, he knew she felt it too. They were just too darn stubborn to admit it.

And now, perhaps it was too late?

It felt so unfair.

If you give me another chance, dear God, I will never let her go. I promise.

He heard footsteps, then a door or hatch opening, and soon felt the presence of someone. A voice came close to him, the same one from earlier.

"Are you awake?"

He nodded. He tried to move, wanting to fight but couldn't. He panted behind the tape.

"Good," she said and touched his hair. "We should fix you up a little because it's showtime, and you'll want to look good for the camera."

Chapter 61

"I NEED to get into room 327."

I stared at the young man behind the glass at the front desk. Billy was with me, ready to roll as soon as I told him to. I had knocked on the door of the room, but no one opened it. I showed the young man my badge and slammed my hand onto the counter to wake him up.

"Did you hear me?"

"Y-yes, but... I don't...."

"No buts," I said. "I have reason to believe there's a crime being committed inside that room. So, if you'll—*please*—help me gain access."

He looked perplexed and glanced toward the phone. "Y-yes, I understand that, but... I need to call...."

"We don't have time to call your supervisor and wake him up. I need to get into that room now. Either you help me, or I will kick the freaking door down myself or use a fire axe to hack through it, and then you'll have the privilege of telling your supervisor why the door is broken and why someone was killed in there on your watch. The choice is yours. What will it be?"

He stared at me, eyes growing wide. Then, he nodded. "O-of course. Let me just…." He leaned down, grabbed a keycard, came out from behind the counter, and cleared his throat nervously.

"Follow me."

We did—into the elevator and up to the third floor. We hurried out, and he rushed to the door, then knocked.

"This is the concierge. Is anyone in there? We need to get inside."

"Already tried that one," I said. "Just with it being the FBI, which you'd think would have more of an impact. Now, please open the door, will you?"

"O-okay."

He slid the key through the reader, and the door clicked open. I pushed past him with an annoyed *thank you*, then rushed inside.

"Matt?"

Billy was right behind me, the camera on his shoulder, capturing every second. I had asked him to come with me in order to get evidence, to get the entire thing on tape, especially if we were to meet the kidnapper and maybe even the killer in there. But so far, we were met by nothing but darkness. I flipped the light switch, then called again.

"Matt? MATT?"

Where is he? He's supposed to be here.

I scanned the room. It had two queen beds, a TV mounted on the wall, a desk, and a chair.

But no Matt.

Panic erupted. Was this the right room? Had I heard the number wrong? I turned to look at Billy, who stuck the camera right in my face—or so it felt. Then my eyes fell on the bathroom. The door was closed. I grabbed the handle, pushed it open, and turned on the light.

I heard a scream and thought it was my own. It wasn't. It was Billy's.

Chapter 62

THEN:

"How can they charge her with murder when it was self-defense?"

Rob looked at his two oldest children. It was his son, Peter, who had asked the question. They were sitting at the dining room table, and Rob explained what was happening. After he had told Janet the news, she had started to cry—just silent tears rolling down her cheeks, but they hadn't stopped. She was sitting in the living room now, staring blankly out the window, picking at the tips of her fingers like she was getting rid of dirt that wasn't there. Rob had given her a Xanax that the doctor had given them for situations like these. She had kept repeating the same phrase over and over again, "I'm a murderer. I'm a murderer."

Rob had told her it wasn't true, that they'd fight this in court, but she wasn't listening to his reasoning.

"That is how they'll see me," she said. "Everyone out there will think that about me."

He had called the children and asked them to come over. The

youngest was still away at college, so she wouldn't be there until the next day.

"There was no weapon," he explained to his grown children. "He was unarmed."

Peter shook his head. "That makes no sense. Didn't Mom say the intruder had a gun?"

Rob looked at his hands. "They never found it. The police searched our house after the incident but never found a gun."

"Didn't you see it?" Peter asked.

Rob shook his head. "No. I never saw any gun."

"But still," Peter continued. "Armed or not. He was an intruder. He broke into our home."

"She knew him," Rob said. His hands shook as he tried to grab the beer in front of him, which his oldest son had given him. He was going to need something stronger soon—like a scotch. But Rob was a light drinker and not very used to hard liquor.

"What?" Peter wrinkled his nose. He looked at his two siblings, who were listening in silence. Then he threw out his hands. "What do you mean she knew him?"

Rob exhaled. "It was the same man—the one that attacked her last time."

"What?" Peter grunted angrily like it was his father's fault—like he had come up with these insane charges. "But even so? He was coming back for more money, right? I mean, that happens a lot, I bet?"

"They're arguing that it was premeditated. She had the bat ready by the door. They're calling it a murder weapon. They're gonna argue that she lured him inside the house to get revenge for what he did to her, and then she attacked him with the bat. His family is determined to prosecute."

"But he broke into the house?"

"They never found any evidence of breaking and entering," Rob said.

"He came through an open window?"

"Yes, that's what we know, but they can't see that he forced himself inside."

"And they believe his family over our mother, the woman he has attacked once before?"

"They're arguing that he was reborn again in prison and became a Christian, that he denied his old ways, plus that he was apparently autistic and mentally ill. He would never attack anyone again, they say. Plus, she didn't stop. Once she had knocked him down, she could have stopped. She could have run away, but she kept beating him down with the bat until he was dead. And she didn't call the police until the next day."

"She was in shock!" Peter argued.

"And so was I," Rob said. "Completely devastated and in shock. But how do you argue this? It's very unlikely they'll win such a case, our lawyer says, so that's the good news. But the prosecution is determined to try out these new laws just implemented with harsher punishment for premeditated murder and manslaughter of an unarmed victim. That's why it's becoming a big deal. It's political. I'm sorry it has come to this, kiddos. All we can do now is support your mother and hope for the best."

Peter was about to say something else but hesitated when seeing his mother standing in the doorway. She was staring at all of them.

"Mom?"

"You all think I'm a murderer, don't you? That's how the world will see me—like I am one of *them*."

Rob rose to his feet. "N-no, honey. Please, don't…."

But it was too late to argue. She had left.

Chapter 63

"WHAT IS THAT?!"

Billy, the cameraman, was screaming behind me. I would like to say that he was overreacting, but anyone would probably have reacted like that when seeing what we did.

"It's a dead body," I said and stared at the tub, where the skeleton was sitting like it had just been taking a bath recently. "And it's been dead quite a while."

Billy forced himself to get over the shock, and with hands shaking, he was filming the skeleton from all angles while I called Fickle and woke him up.

"What are we looking at?" he asked with a deep yawn when he showed up half an hour later, along with several police officers who started blocking off the room. The techs were going to come soon and start securing evidence. Hopefully, whoever had planted this body here had left something behind for me to find. I had a feeling he had, if not by accident, then because this person wanted me to follow a lead. His lead. I was tired of being played with.

"You tell me," I said, showing him to the bathroom.

"Geez," he said.

"My guess is it's another one of the missing women," I said. "Someone is playing games with us, I believe."

"About that," Fickle said. "There's something I need to tell you."

"What?"

He pulled me aside and spoke in a low voice so the camera wouldn't record what he told me.

"I was working all night, and just as I left, I got the results from the DNA test. It did match a person in our register, but not who you thought it was."

"What do you mean?"

He shook his head. "It wasn't a woman. It was a man."

I paused to let this sink in.

"Really?"

He nodded. "His name was Malcolm Astor. He's been arrested before on trafficking of heroin charges."

My heart dropped. "There goes my main suspect. How... I don't... but the hip replacement?"

"He was an older man. He had one done five years ago."

I couldn't believe this. I couldn't stop thinking about poor Scott and the fact that he had falsely been told it was his mother's body.

"I'll be...."

I grabbed my face with both hands. I couldn't figure out what was up or down in this case. If Astor hadn't taken the women out to sea and killed them, then who had? And who was replacing these bodies for me to find? And most importantly, where was Matt?

I left Fickle to do his work, then returned to the bedroom when a Miami PD officer approached me.

"Agent Thomas?"

"Yes?"

"They need you to call the station. It's urgent."

Chapter 64

SHE WAS IN TROUBLE. Allyssa knew she was, and she also knew she had to do something. No one could help her but herself, and she knew precisely how. She couldn't let her family know who she was or, even worse—what she was. Her past had caught up with her, and it was time to punch back.

I'm not going to take this lying down.

She dragged the heavy body across the ground. It was still the middle of the night, and there were hours to sunrise. She had time to get rid of the evidence—to delete her tracks.

Allyssa grunted and pulled at his shoulders, but she got tired and sat down. Why was this guy so heavy? She grabbed his legs instead and turned him around, then pulled them. It went easier this way. She pulled him down the stairs, his head bumping on each and every one of them. She felt like apologizing but told herself she was being an idiot.

It's not like he can feel anything.

"Come on, just a little farther."

She said the words out loud as a pep talk to herself. She was so tired, her arms hurting from carrying, pushing, and pulling this body.

"You can do it. You're almost there."

She looked ahead of her and exhaled. Then, she grabbed his legs and started to pull again. She really didn't have a lot farther to go, and then it would all be over. She dragged him a few feet more, then had to stop. She fell on her knees, catching her breath. She looked at his face. She had wrapped him in a blanket from the car in case anyone saw her, but now that she dropped him down again, his head popped out. She grabbed the blanket and tried to cover his face. The last thing she needed was to see it. Blood had seeped through the blanket from the wound in his abdomen, where she had stabbed him.

"I'm sorry," she whispered, pulling the blanket over his head. "I'm so, so sorry. I only did this because I had to."

She thought about her baby, Kaylee, and almost started to cry. She couldn't bear the thought of being unable to see her start preschool, graduate, or one day get married. It was all for her that she had to do it—for her daughter's sake.

You can't give up now. You have to finish this.

Allyssa grabbed the legs again and started to pull. Fueled by the thought of her daughter, she found new strength and moved the body all the way to the dock. She put him down once again so she could breathe, then looked nervously around her, praying no one would see her.

Then, she grabbed his legs again and pushed him into the water headfirst. The body slid into the murky waters like it was weightless, but the rocks she had put in his pockets would hopefully make him sink to the bottom. She looked at it nervously and couldn't see it anymore. She hoped sharks and gators would get rid of it but worried someone would find it first.

You can't think like that. Think positive thoughts. The ocean is your friend.

For a second, she suddenly panicked and thought it was all

wrong, that she should have buried him instead, that someone would find him, but by then, it was too late. She bent down to look for it, but the body was gone.

Chapter 65

"I HAVE a man on the line. He says he needs to talk to you and that it is urgent. He says he has information about the missing women."

"Okay, put him through."

I had walked into the hotel hallway while Fickle did his job. It was still dark out and the middle of the night. I felt so tired but also deeply worried about Matt. I knew I wouldn't be able to sleep until I found him. Whoever had him liked to play games, and I was anxiously awaiting my next clue while trying to figure this person out and what their next move would be. Until now, I had been sure we were chasing Malcolm Astor, who was trying to hide his drug trafficking business, but now that he was dead, I had no idea what I was looking at anymore. It felt like I was back at square one, making me very uncomfortable. It gave this person all the power. They were in charge, and all I could do was follow suit.

To keep Matt alive.

"H-ello? Is this Agent Thomas?" The voice on the other end was frantic, hectic almost. This man was obviously desperate.

"This is she."

"My name is Joe Fischer. I need to talk to you about those four missing women. I understand you're the head detective on the case?"

"Yes."

"I... I think I have some information you need."

I found a chair and sat down in the hallway. I took out my notepad to write down anything important that came up. He could still turn out to be some drunk lunatic.

"What kind of information?"

"It's my wife. I'm worried about her."

"Why are you worried about her?"

"Because she's missing. She left earlier tonight to get ice cream at the gas station but never came home."

"I see, and now you're worried that she's missing like those other women?" I asked, thinking this didn't sound like it was worth my time.

"N-No, no, that's not why I'm calling."

"Okay, why are you calling?"

"Sh-she... there's something strange going on with her. I don't know... but she knew the woman that was found dead. She... she had her necklace and a picture of them together when they were younger."

Now, he was piquing my interest. "I see, but I'm sure these women knew a lot of people when they were younger?"

"I know; I'm just worried... because she was being weird about it and not telling me, and now that she is missing, I'm worried that she has done something."

I wrinkled my forehead. "Done something? Like what?"

"Something stupid."

"And why would she do something stupid?"

"I don't know... I'm not sure I even know who she is anymore."

"Listen, I get that...."

He interrupted me. "She has another name."

"Excuse me?"

"When I say I don't know her anymore, I mean I literally don't even know her real name. I found an old driver's license from Kentucky where her name was Kristen. Kristen Thomasson."

Chapter 66

THEN:

Where did she go? Where did Mom go?

Peter rose to his feet and wanted to follow her, but his dad stopped him by grabbing his arm.

"Give her some space. She probably just needs a few minutes. I'll go talk to her once she has calmed down a little."

"Shouldn't we try and...."

Rob shook his head. "I'll talk to her in a little bit."

Peter backed down and sat in his chair with a deep sigh. He shook his head. "I can't believe this is happening. What if Mom is going to jail?"

"Let's not jump to conclusions here. We need to keep calm," Rob said. "All of us. I know it's a lot to ask, but it's all we can do."

He looked at all three children in the kitchen. The two younger ones had barely spoken a word. They let their big brother do the talking. However, Rob saw a few tears leave their eyes, which were wiped away quickly, which broke his heart. These kids were in their twenties and shouldn't be worried about their mother. They should be out there grabbing life—living it.

Not sitting here, worrying their mom might go to jail for defending herself—in her own freaking home. What had this world come to? Protecting the criminals over the innocent? Believing she could ever have hurt anyone without a good reason?

You saw her. Pounding on that dead body. You didn't see any gun.

Rob shook his head. No, he refused to believe it. All this made him doubt his own judgment. He had to trust his wife. Of course, he did.

But she hadn't been herself since the first attack. She was obsessed with getting revenge and believed the justice system had failed her. What if she did take matters into her own hands?

No, he had to stop thinking like that. Janet was his beloved wife and didn't deserve to go to jail.

"I'm sure our attorney will be able to help us," he told the children, but just as much to calm himself. "He seemed very convinced over the phone that this probably wouldn't even make it to trial. I don't think we need to worry so much. Okay?"

But he also said that it might. The prosecutor was trying to make a career of these types of cases.

Rob forced a smile, and the children seemed comforted by his words. They nodded, and Peter even pulled out half a smile.

"Now, we need to focus on what we *can* do: help your mom out around the house. I'm gonna need you guys to take over with the laundry, cleaning, and cooking for a little while. I don't want her to have to think about all that stuff while this is happening. And I will be busy, too, taking care of her and the case."

Peter nodded. "Of course. We'll make a schedule and come by to help as much as we can."

"Good. You guys are amazing children, and what I want to do next is to…."

But Rob never managed to finish the sentence. He was interrupted by the sound of a gun going off.

They all stared at one another, and panic erupted amongst them. They got up so fast that chairs tumbled to the floor. They ran for the living room, where they saw first the blood, then their mother and wife still sitting in her chair, head slumped, and finally, the gun in her lifeless hand, which slowly slid to the floor below with a thud.

Chapter 67

I ASKED Joe to send me a recent picture of his wife, who went by the name Allyssa now, and he did. I looked at it on my phone, and even though she had dyed her hair black and gotten some filler in her lips, I could tell by her eyes that this woman was, in fact, the missing Kristen Thomasson. How she had been able to walk around in public for the past three years and have no one recognize her was beyond me. But it wasn't unusual. I just couldn't believe that she was actually alive.

What did this mean?

Did *she* kill the others? Marley? Malcolm?

I exhaled, puzzled at this. Why would this woman suddenly start making the bodies appear for me to find, creating this odd game of hers if she had spent the past three years hiding and actually getting away with this?

It didn't make much sense.

Did she maybe want to be caught?

Sometimes, they did. Sometimes, they couldn't live with themselves and had to come clean somehow but didn't know how. This could be a way. Sometimes, they realized they wanted to kill again, making them want to be stopped. It wasn't unusual behavior for a serial killer.

I stared at the photo. Was that what I was looking at? Was this housewife a serial killer?

I had seen stranger things.

The door to the hotel room opened, and Fickle came out. He seemed to be searching for someone and lifted his hand when he saw me.

"There you are."

He approached me, holding something in his hand. I guessed it had to be my next clue.

Here we go.

"I found this inside the skeleton. It was stuffed between the ribs and took a few minutes to get out," he said. "I don't really know what to make of it, but I think it could be important for you."

I nodded and looked at him. "Let me guess. The marina, right?"

He looked at me, surprised. "I... I guess you're right. It's a picture of a boat. How did you know?"

I grabbed the small picture with a yacht on it out of his hand and started to walk away.

"I'm slowly getting to know this person," I said and waved.

He was still looking at me like I was insane. I pressed the button for the elevator, then yelled at him as the doors closed after I pressed the lobby button inside.

"I'll explain later."

"You better."

I looked at my watch and realized it would soon become day, and the sun was about to rise. I was wary of rushing to the marina and seeing what was waiting for me next.

I feared it was Matt.

Chapter 68

IF ANYONE HURTS MATT, *I will kill them.*

I was speeding across town, heart throbbing in my chest. I didn't know or understand what this person wanted from me or why we had to go through all these hoops, but somewhere in this, there was a message that this person was trying to tell me.

I just couldn't figure out what that message was.

Why go through all the trouble of relocating the bodies?

Why kidnap Matt?

It almost seemed personal—like this person was targeting me. But why? Did I know this person?

I took a right and ran a yellow light, then skidded sideways before regaining control of the car. I felt this deep worry and unease inside while trying to figure out what the heck this was all about. I had nothing to do with this case before now. Was it because of the TV show? Did this person want to be famous? To be seen?

Or was it something else?

I spotted the marina in front of me, then drove down to the parking lot and dropped off the car. I got out and ran to the docks, the picture of the yacht clutched in my hand. The yacht was named

Petra, and I immediately tried to find it, running down every dock and looking at the names of all the boats.

But *Petra* wasn't there.

I growled loudly and was so annoyed. What was the entire point of making me come down here if the freaking boat wasn't even here!

I was getting tired of these little games. What was even the point of them? Just to drive me nuts?

I turned around with the intention of walking back to the car when I spotted something in the water. The sun was rising slowly, and the rays of sunlight were hitting whatever it was between the cloud cover. But I didn't need much light to know exactly what I was looking at. The way it bobbed up and down beneath the surface told me everything I needed to know.

I had seen a dead body in water before.

My heart throbbed, and I ran toward it on the dock beside me with a small shriek stuck in my throat. I tried to reach down and grab it, but my arms weren't long enough. The body was sort of lodged underneath the dock, possibly stuck to one of the pillars somehow. I jumped into the water and grabbed it, then pulled it toward the shore. Whoever it was, was wearing a blue T-shirt, just like Matt. The realization made me panic.

Someone had seen me jump in, and I heard yelling; then, people came running to help. A man jumped into the water with me and helped me lift the body out of the water while two other men grabbed the body by the arms and pulled it up onto the dock.

Panting frantically, I was pulled up next and then hurried to the body. One of the men shook his head as he tried to find a pulse. I couldn't see the body's face, and fearing it was Matt, I hurried to it, then knelt next to it. I turned his head to face me, gasped, and pulled back in shock.

Chapter 69

IT TOOK FOREVER before anything else happened. Matt was in the darkness, shivering in fear, not knowing what would happen.

And then the hatch opened again, and someone came to him. He could hear their movements and sense that it was daylight out since a small ray of sunlight slipped underneath the tape covering his eyes.

Matt tried to scream, but the tape reduced his efforts to nothing but muffled sounds.

HEEELP!

The person came close and touched his hair again. Hands were grabbing at him, touching him.

"Such gorgeous hair," she said. "And a handsome face to go with it."

He tried to pull away, but she grabbed his hair and pulled it hard. "No use in squirming," she hissed.

Matt grunted behind the tape, then, as she put her head close to his and he sensed she was right next to him, he slammed his head into hers. The woman screamed and stumbled back.

"What the he…?"

But Matt was fast. He shot upright, lifted his tied-together feet, and kicked toward where he believed she was. He hit her instantly, hard. He heard her shriek; then, a thud followed as she fell to the floor.

Then there was nothing.

Did she pass out?

He fumbled with his tied-up hands. They were strapped behind his back. By twisting and turning them, he managed to get the tape loosened so he could move his hands and fingers. He kept wriggling them, stretching the tape. Then, he fell to his knees and bent back far enough for his hands to grab around the tape tying his legs together. Breathing hard, he felt for an opening and managed to grab onto one, then pulled it. The tape started to come apart, and he pulled again, then had to stop to breathe and bend forward for a few seconds because his back was hurting before continuing. He managed to grab the tape again, then ripped it open, and soon his feet and legs were untied, and he could stand to his feet. He stumbled forward toward the sparse light he could see underneath the tape. He bumped into a set of stairs and hurt himself. He went up the stairs carefully, one step at a time. The sun hit his face and warmed him. He could hear birds.

Seagulls.

Where am I?

Fumbling with his arms still behind his back, he touched the wall behind him, then walked, touching the slick wall until his hand touched something. It felt like an edge, but he was unsure if it was sharp enough. He gave it a try. He put the tape on top of it, then started to move it. Grunting with the effort, he filed the tape back and forth, back and forth, until it suddenly sprang open with a snap.

He had to hurry. He lifted his free hands, then grabbed the tape around his head and unwrapped it. Seconds later, he was able to open his eyes slowly. The light was blinding, and he blinked a few times to see better. As his sight gradually returned, he realized he was surrounded by blue.

He was on a boat in the middle of the ocean, and no land was in sight. Behind him, he heard footsteps coming up the stairs.

Chapter 70

IT WASN'T MATT I was looking at, but it was someone I knew.

"Mark," I said, holding my mouth. "Mark Benton."

"The pastor," a voice said, coming up next to me. I turned to look at him. He was dripping wet, and I realized this was the guy that had jumped into the water to help me.

"He would always sing and pray for me," he said. "Every morning when I came here. I kind of liked it."

"Wait a minute," I said, staring at the man beside me. "You're Malcolm Astor? But that's not... that's not possible?"

"Henry Astor, but close enough," he said with a slight smile. "I'm his brother. We're twins."

"Twins? Huh."

It made sense. That's how Mark, "the pastor," thought he saw Malcolm on the marina and waved at him. Only it wasn't him. It was his brother.

"I only learned of his death yesterday," he said. "The police called me and said they had found his body. He went missing three years ago, and we never knew what happened to him. He was involved with drugs and bad people, and we assumed he had gotten into trouble."

"And that's why you never reported him missing to the police. Because then they'd find out."

Henry nodded. "Not a day has passed without me wondering what happened to him. I took over his charter business and have been running it for him until he returned. I guess that's not happening."

I scoffed and nodded, then called the station and reported the finding of Pastor Mark. I stared at his lifeless body, then realized he had been stabbed in the abdomen before being thrown into the water.

Just like the others. Was this the work of the same killer? Was this person removing evidence because Mark had spoken to us and told us he saw them together? Maybe it wasn't a clue, I realized.

I looked at the picture in my hand while sirens wailed in the distance and my colleagues were approaching the scene. I looked up at Henry, then showed him the picture.

"Do you recognize this boat?"

He nodded. "Yes, as a matter of fact, I do. It is usually docked over there, but this morning, it was gone when I got here. They must have left early, which is odd since they rarely leave the dock."

I stared toward the horizon and the blue water while biting my cheek, trying to assemble this puzzle. I had to figure out what this was all about—for Matt's sake. And fast, before he was in trouble I couldn't get him out of. My thoughts kept circling around Kristen Thomasson and the fact that she was still alive, and her husband was worried about her and what she might do.

Something stupid.

As I stood there and stared toward the ocean, something struck me—a thought that led to another thought, and suddenly, a picture was painted. As I realized who the killer was, I felt so terrified that I started to shake. I knew Matt's life was in great danger if I was right. And the worst of it was that it was all because of me.

Chapter 71

AS SOON AS my colleagues from Miami PD got there, I asked them to help me get ahold of a speedboat. Luckily, they had one docked at this very marina, and one of the officers was used to patrolling by boat, so he got in with me and started it up. I showed him the picture of the *Petra* and told him that's what we were looking for.

We took off.

It was a windy day, and as soon as we left the marina, salt water splashed us from the side, soaking my clothes and face.

We made it far from the marina, yet the *Petra* was nowhere to be seen. And I had no idea what direction they could have gone. The ocean suddenly seemed endless, and maybe my idea was not as bright as it had seemed earlier.

"Should we alert the coastguard?" Officer Jameson asked, yelling to overpower the loud engine noise.

"I asked the sergeant to do it," I yelled back. "But it might take a while before they get their chopper in the air. I'm not sure we have that kind of time."

The truth was, I wouldn't be able just to stay behind and do nothing. The man I dearly loved—and the father of my child—was in danger, and I wanted to help him. No matter the cost.

I'd take a bullet for him any day.

I realized in that instant how deep my feelings for him went. We had been through so much stuff, and we had given up. But had it been too fast? Had we given up too easily?

Was our love worth another try?

I sighed deeply, realizing I might never know the answer to that question. Not if I didn't find him.

Why hadn't I seen this coming? Why didn't I realize this person was trying to hurt me a long time ago when the first body turned up?

I should have. It was so obvious.

And now, it might cost me the love of my life.

You can't think like that. You simply can't.

I focused on the task ahead, trying to calm my heavily beating heart. I had to focus; I had to find him. I simply had to.

I stared through the binoculars, searching the horizon for any signs of a boat. And just like that, I spotted one. I tried to hold the binoculars still enough to see the name on it, but the big waves made it difficult. Finally, I found it and could read it.

PETRA.

"Over there," I said and pointed so Jameson could see. "To your starboard side. That's the boat we're looking for."

He spotted it and directed the speedboat toward it, bumping along on the waves. It was a good thing I wasn't prone to seasickness. I'm sure this weather would have caused that, but I had no time to feel sick. I had to save Matt, no matter what. I had to save him, so I could tell him I loved him. Cheesy? Sure. But it was the truth, and I was sick of hiding it, sick of pretending and lying to myself.

I just prayed that I wasn't too late.

Chapter 72

I SPOTTED him as we came closer. My shoulders came down, and I felt myself breathe normally again. Right there on the main deck, I could see Matt. He was just standing there, looking at us without moving.

I waved.

"Matt! Matt!"

Jameson slowed down as we approached the yacht. I felt tears in my eyes as I continuously waved and yelled his name, but he didn't wave back. As a matter of fact, he didn't move a muscle.

Something's not right.

I lowered my arms and placed a hand on the grip of my gun instead. The way Matt looked at us told me he was in trouble, and as we came closer, I realized what it was. He had a gun pointed at his back, held by a woman behind him. She yelled at us.

"Throw your weapons overboard, or he will die."

I stared at her while Jameson slowed to a halt. My eyes met hers, and I could feel myself getting agitated. I was pissed, to put it mildly. Who the heck did she think she was? For a second, I considered pulling my gun and trying to shoot her, but it was a risk, and the way she hid behind Matt, I wouldn't be able to get a clean shot.

I couldn't do it.

I pulled the gun out by the grip, then held it up in the air before tossing it in the water. Jameson did the same. We both held our hands over our heads.

"Can we come aboard?" I asked.

"Please, do," the woman yelled back. "I've been waiting for you."

I signaled for Jameson to get the boat closer, and he did. I grabbed the railing and jumped onboard, then hurried up the stairs to the main deck. As I did, the woman looked at me briefly and smiled.

And that's when I knew.

She pulled the trigger. The gun went off with a loud noise, piercing through my heart. Blood spurted on the deck from his chest. Matt jerked forward, and she pushed him into the ocean.

I screamed.

"I don't need him anymore," she said.

I ran toward her and where he had been, then stared into the ocean where his body was floating face down.

No, no, no, please, say it isn't true. Please, God.

I got ready to jump in when she stopped me. She pointed the gun at me. "Oh, no, you don't. Not if you ever want to see your children again. And that cop still in the boat, he doesn't touch him either; you hear me?"

I stared at the lifeless body in the water, barely breathing. I felt so useless, so angry and scared at the same time, then I turned to face her.

"What do you want from me? You've been targeting me from the beginning, haven't you?"

She smiled. "Yes. From the moment you killed my mother."

Chapter 73

"I SHOULD HAVE REALIZED it was you. I should have recognized you."

"I was surprised you didn't," she said.

"You were giving me clues all along. The bodies turning up conveniently, right when we got here, and very close to where we were. I knew something was wrong with that picture. How did you find them?"

"On a diving trip about a year ago, almost by coincidence. My boyfriend and I were scuba diving down here, and we went out on a boat. We jumped in and dove down, then saw the yacht, or what was left of it. All the bodies were lodged inside, on the deck below. My boyfriend helped me get them out of the water and to a storage room in the harbor. We did it in the middle of the night and wrapped them up in blankets, so no one could see what they were."

"How did you know who they were?" I asked.

She shrugged. "A little research taught me that four women had gone missing in Miami three years ago. I quickly traced them to the marina and found Pastor Mark, who told me he saw them go out on a boat. It was good old police work and what the detectives should have done from the beginning. But you know how lazy they are and how freaking imbecilic the police are. They can't even find a stupid gun."

I exhaled. We had been through this a million times. "I told you; we searched the house the best we could and didn't find it."

"But my mom found it easily and used it to shoot herself."

"That's not my fault. That's not fair to assume."

"You were the detective on the case. You were investigating the attack on my mother in her own home and couldn't find the darn gun. If you had, she would be here today. She wouldn't have been accused of murdering the man who attacked her. They wouldn't have said she was luring him in for revenge and beat him to death. He had a gun. That's why she did it. But no, because you never found the gun, she thought she was going to jail for defending herself and ended up shooting herself—with the very gun you and your people couldn't find. How's that for irony?"

"You know it has been tormenting me for years," I said.

"Not enough even to remember my face," she said.

"You were young, only nineteen back then. You've changed a lot," I said. "That's not fair."

"Well, life isn't fair, is it?" she hissed, swinging the gun at me. "I had to learn that the hard way."

All I could think about was Matt in the water and getting him out of there and to a hospital. Was he dead? Was it too late?

But I also needed to get home to my children. I knew this woman wasn't kidding around. She would kill me, and it was probably her intention.

"Listen, you tried to sue the police department; you complained about me, and I was reprimanded by my chief and had to take a suspension. I'm sorry for what happened to you. I truly am. I know I was in charge, so, yes, I am to blame for not finding the gun. But I didn't kill your mother."

She lifted the gun with an angry movement and walked closer to me. I backed up, raising my hands in the air.

"No, you killed her; you were the one who is to blame for every-thing that happened. I came home from college right after my mom killed herself. I never even got to say goodbye. You drove her to it. You ruined everything. I lost both my parents within a week just because you didn't do your job properly."

Chapter 74

"BOTH YOUR PARENTS?" I stared at her, baffled. "What do you mean?"

"When my mom shot herself, my dad couldn't deal with life anymore," she said. "He got scared of living in their house and got up at every creaking sound, every floorboard that made a noise. He would get so scared, thinking it was an intruder. We talked about getting him a dog but never got around to it."

I frowned. "What happened to him?"

She was fighting her tears now. "I was going to go back to my college and went grocery shopping for him. I came back home with all the things I had bought. I found him inside on the floor where my mother had died."

"H-how did he die?"

"They call it broken-heart syndrome," she said. "Or stress-induced cardiomyopathy. His heart simply stopped beating due to the grief he suffered."

"I didn't know that," I said.

"We were all orphaned within a week. Just because you didn't do

239

your job." She said the last part with a loud growl. I sensed the deep anger inside of her and was overwhelmed with guilt, even though it was almost ten years ago. I had been beating myself up over this for years, and now I was again.

"I'm so, so sorry."

"Shut up! Shut up!"

The gun was vibrating in front of my face, and I stared down its barrel.

"What do you want from me?" I asked.

Her nostrils were flaring, and she stared at me for a few seconds before she answered, "I want you to smile for the cameras. I've placed Go-Pro cameras several places on this boat, so we could get this from more than one angle."

I turned and spotted one attached to the railing. "This is why you wanted me to do the TV show? I should have known it from the beginning. Lydia was your mother's middle name, right? Janet Lydia Carey."

"I wanted the world to see you fail. I wanted them to realize how big of a fraud you really are. Once the bodies were discovered, there was no way you could figure out what happened to them or even how they got there, and I was right. And we have it all on camera. How moronic you look, running around looking for clues and not figuring it out. You've won awards and written books, and people look up to you like you're some big-shot detective and profiler, but in reality, you're none of that. You're an imposter, Eva Rae Thomas. And soon, the world will realize that."

"But I found you," I said.

That made her laugh. "I led you here, and you know it. I wanted this to be the end scene of our show. Me—the superior—shooting you. The world seeing that I—a small-town girl—am way smarter than the big-shot FBI profiler. I outsmarted you. And it cost you your life and your boyfriend's."

I swallowed as she pushed the gun closer.

"Listen, there's no need to…."

She was done listening to me. She shook her head.

"No. No more. It ends here. Smile for the cameras, Eva Rae Thomas. This is your last chance. Ten seconds until showtime."

Chapter 75

SHE WAS BITING HER NAILS. Allyssa—or Kristen, as her real name was—had heard everything happening up on the deck while contemplating what she should do. After dumping the pastor's body in the water, she had entered a boat docked at the marina and hid below deck, thinking this was a good way for her to escape. She didn't care where they went as long as she got away. She was hoping for the Caribbean, but anywhere would do.

She had watched as the woman had shot the guy, and now she was holding a gun to a woman's head. She recognized her from TV as the FBI agent working on the case—their case.

She heard the woman holding the gun say, "Smile for the cameras."

She's gonna kill her too. What do I do?

Kristen panicked. She felt terrified to the core. If this woman shot the FBI agent, then what would happen next? The police would arrive, and they'd find Kristen onboard. She couldn't go back. She needed to get out of there.

You gotta take control of the situation. Take over the darn boat.

She thought about the many possible scenarios and shivered

slightly, worried that there was no way this could end well. But if she didn't do something, she'd either end up dead or in prison. She couldn't let either of those things happen. She had come too far for that.

Just do it.

The waves crashed against the yacht's sides and made her walk wobbly. Yet she made it to the bottom of the stairs while watching what was happening on the deck above. She remembered the last time she had been on a boat, and the memory made her shiver in fear. They had all thought they were just going there to party. Malcolm Astor had promised them a fun night out on the water.

Yet Kristen had been the only one who came back alive.

The yacht had burned and taken their bodies down with it. She had never thought she would have to deal with any of them again—with any part of this story.

But now, it had come back to haunt her.

GO!

She scanned the area, looking for anything she could use as a weapon, then grabbed the big fender the size of a small child and stormed up the stairs. She swung the fender at the woman holding the gun so hard that she tumbled to the ground, and the gun fell into the water.

Then, Kristen jumped the woman and started to let the punches fall on her face and chest. Blood spurted on her shirt, but she continued regardless until the woman below lay completely still.

Chapter 76

WHAT ON EARTH?

I screamed when the fender came toward us out of nowhere. I pulled back so I wouldn't get hit when it slammed into Lydia and knocked her to the deck. Seconds later, a woman was on top of her, beating down on her.

I stared at the scene, paralyzed. Then I decided it was now or never and jumped in the water.

I grabbed Matt by the shoulders and pulled him toward Jameson, who helped me get him out of the water and into the police boat.

"Take him to the hospital. Hurry," I said. "Then send people to get us."

"But what about you?"

"I need to finish this," I said, letting go of the boat. I climbed aboard the yacht again, then ran to the deck, where I grabbed the woman and pulled her off Lydia. Panting, we fell to the deck.

"That's enough. She's not moving anymore."

As I finally saw the woman's face properly, I realized it was Allyssa, or rather Kristen Thomasson—the fourth member of the group. I sat up straight and moved my hair from my face when she looked at me.

"It was you, wasn't it?" I asked.

"What do you mean?"

"You killed the others. How else could you have survived?"

She looked away. "The yacht caught on fire. I jumped in the water."

I stared at her, then shook my head. "No. Then you would have called for help. You've been hiding for three years, taking a different identity, starting a new life. What happened? Why did you kill them?"

Kristen stared at me, first defiantly, then she began to cry.

"I'm guessing it was an accident?" I asked.

She nodded with a sniffle. "I loved her. I was in love with her. I told her that, and then she freaked out."

"Who?"

She looked up at me. "Marley. I told her I was in love with her. She laughed. She humiliated me. She said she wasn't a *disgusting* lesbian."

"Is that why you killed her?"

"I didn't mean to. I just... I got so angry. I grabbed a knife, one of those fishing ones lying around the boat because it was often chartered for fishing trips," Kristen said as she clenched her fists in anger.

"When I came back down, she had told Janice. They laughed at me. Pat had fallen asleep up on top, so she didn't hear what was happening. But those two... those bitches, they laughed at me. Even Malcolm did. He said he'd like to watch us together. But they were having fun because of me. I just... well, it wasn't true. That's what I yelled at them. We had been together many times before, Marley and me. But she wouldn't acknowledge it. She wouldn't admit to it. I was ready to leave my husband for her. But she just... mocked me."

"You stabbed her in the stomach?" I asked.

"I didn't mean to kill her. It just happened. I waited until they had all fallen asleep, then I did it. And then I cried. I held her in my arms and cried because she was the love of my life. I took her necklace as my only memory—that and a picture I had of us on my old Hotmail that I was able to access later—one she had sent me a long time ago."

"And the others?"

"Once I realized what I had done, I knew I could never go back. I killed them all, one after another, while wearing a scuba mask, so they wouldn't know it was me—one after another. Then, I started a fire in the kitchen, knowing the yacht would sink with all of them inside. I believed it would cover my tracks. I found a flotation device and sat on it, using a paddle to get back to shore. It took me an entire day and night because we were so far out, but I finally managed to get back to the beach down south of Miami. I think I slept for two days on that beach afterward. I had taken everyone's phones and credit cards, so they couldn't track them and placed them in a trash bin by the Seven-Eleven. I wanted the police to find them there so they'd think we had all just taken off voluntarily—or at least confuse them about where to look for us. I broke into a home nearby, stole clothes, a driver's license, and money, showered, and then entered the world as a new woman. I met Joe in a coffee shop a few weeks later, when I had rented a small place not far away, and we fell in love. We had a baby, and everything was good until you showed up—all of you—making that obnoxious TV show."

"And I'm guessing you killed Pastor Mark as well?" I asked. "To cover your tracks?"

She nodded. "I had read on a Facebook page that follows the TV crew that they were talking to him and that supposedly he had seen the women board a yacht. I knew I had to get rid of him before it was too late and they found the yacht on the bottom of the ocean. The walls were closing in, you know? I was getting scared."

"And then you thought you could escape by boat, hiding on the

Petra but didn't know you had unwittingly become part of the show's final act."

She exhaled deeply. Then she looked up at me with a mischievous grin. "Now, all I have to do is get rid of you and then get this boat to the Caribbean."

She lifted her fist and slammed it into my face, knocking me back. Then she stood above me, grabbed me by the shoulders, and dragged me toward the bow.

"It's okay; you'll probably just drown," she said, then pulled me closer to the edge. "Or be eaten by a shark."

As she stepped closer to the stern, she put her foot inside the anchor chain. Seeing that, I took a chance. This was it—my last chance if I wanted to see my children again. I fought my way out of her grip by kicking her first and then pulling away. I then pulled the handle on the anchor, and the chain started to drop down, spinning so fast that it caught her leg in it, and she was stuck. Kristen screamed loudly as her leg was ripped to blood, and I got to my feet, then hurried to stop the chain from dropping more.

"Help me," she said. "I'm stuck."

Now, it was my turn to smile. I could hear the chopper in the distance and knew it had to be the coastguard. Jameson had to have directed them to our location.

"Oh, I will unstick you… in a little while."

Kristen groaned in pain and tried to move but couldn't. I stared at the cameras that Lydia had put up and thanked her in secret for doing so, as it would now serve as evidence and hopefully get both of them put away for a very long time.

Meanwhile, all I could think about was Matt and whether or not he made it. Had I lost him for good? Or was there still hope?

Epilogue
ONE WEEK LATER

I HATED WEARING BLACK. The only good thing about it was that it made me look slimmer. But it always made me think that someone had died, and in this case, it was true.

"That was a beautiful speech," my daughter, Christine, said as she came up to me. She hugged me tightly. "I'm so sorry, Mom."

I took a deep breath and smelled my daughter's hair like I used to when she was a young child. It always made me feel calm. My mom was standing in the far corner of the room, holding Angel in her arms. Even she was wearing a black dress. I thought putting a small child in a black dress was morbid, but my mom insisted.

"They might as well learn the proper etiquette from the beginning," she argued.

I didn't have the strength to argue back. I was exhausted from planning this entire funeral and dealing with everything else.

"It's okay," I said to Christine. "He died a hero, and he saved many lives. Today, we honor him and the life he led."

"But what about Elijah and Angel?" Christine said. "They're gonna miss him."

I looked toward Elijah in his little black suit. He was Matt's son from an earlier relationship, and I didn't really know him that well. Still, I cared deeply for him and wanted to be there for him if he needed me.

"They'll be okay," I said and kissed her cheek. "Now, make sure there are enough eggrolls, or get some from the kitchen."

She took off, and my sister Sydney came over to me. She kissed my cheek. "I'm sorry for your loss."

"He was a good man," I said. "I owe him a lot."

"Why do you owe him a lot?" Matt said, coming up behind me. He still had his arm in a sling after being shot in the shoulder, but the bullet had gone straight through, so he would be okay after a little physical therapy. He handed me a plate of chicken wings, and I ate one, feeling starved.

"Because your uncle was always so nice to me when I was a child," I said. "And because he left you a good sum of money that you have so generously donated to fix up my house and even built an addition to it, now that you and Elijah will be living there again."

"True, he was a good guy," Matt said. "And a war hero. And a former police officer. But he had been sick for the past several years. To be honest, it was hard to watch him wither away like that, and I think it's good that he finally found peace."

I kissed Matt on the lips and put my head on his shoulder. Per the doctor's orders, he couldn't do much, so I was in charge of helping his mother make the funeral arrangements. Now, I was exhausted. Between finishing up the case and getting a confession from Kristen Thomasson from her hospital bed, where she had her leg amputated, and this, I was ready to sleep for a week. All the recordings from the TV show had been confiscated as evidence, and the network washed its hands of the entire thing, saying they'll never air it. I felt the worst for Tara because she had to realize her mom wasn't who she thought she was. She was the only one who got her mother back, but at what cost? She had to face the others after realizing that her mother had murdered their mothers. Divers had found the wreck and the body of Scott's mom, Janice, and Mike's mom Pat. They were still down there, as Lydia had only moved two bodies, thinking they were two of the mothers and not realizing that one of them was Malcolm Astor, the guy who had taken them out on his boat to party, not knowing it would be his last voyage.

I had told Matt I loved him as soon as he woke up in the hospital bed after surgery. I told him I never wanted to be without him again—that whatever problems we had, we could work them out if we both decided to.

Luckily, he agreed.

And then, I told him I was furious with him for betraying me and telling the TV crew all those details, and he said he was sorry. He was worried they'd sue us; that's why he did it.

I forgave him.

I grabbed his hand in mine and held it tight, then looked at my children. Alex was playing with the food, throwing eggrolls across the room. He hit an elderly lady in the back, and the eggroll got stuck in her hair. I pretended he wasn't my child, then turned my face and kissed Matt.

"Let's elope," I said.

"We could get on a boat? Sail away into the sunset?"

That made me laugh. "I think it will be a while before I go on a boat again. Maybe we should try something else? Something less dangerous, like skydiving."

THE END

Afterword

Dear Reader,

Thank you for purchasing *Too Pretty to Die* (Eva Rae Thomas #13). The idea for this book came to me when going on a privately chartered cruise with a bunch of my friends to the British Virgin Islands. I kept thinking, what if one of us decided to murder everyone else onboard and then burned and sank the boat? We would never be found. I know; I have a crazy, twisted mind, but that's who I am. The setting of a luxury yacht was just very compelling for a mystery.

The story of someone charged with murder for killing an intruder wasn't taken out of the blue. Here's a story that I used to inspire me:

https://www.theguardian.com/world/2014/apr/29/minnesota-man-guilty-murder-teenage-intruders-byron-smith

Finally, I want you to know that I am extremely happy for all your support. It's what makes me keep writing.

Don't forget to leave a review if possible.

Take care,

Willow

About the Author

Willow Rose is a multi-million-copy best-selling Author and an Amazon ALL-star Author of more than 90 novels.

Several of her books have reached the top 10 of ALL books on Amazon in the US, UK, and Canada. She has sold more than three million books all over the world.

She writes Mystery, Thriller, Paranormal, Romance, Suspense, Horror, Supernatural thrillers, and Fantasy.

Willow's books are fast-paced, nail-biting, page-turners with twists you won't see coming. That's why her fans call her The Queen of Scream.

Willow lives on Florida's Space Coast with her husband and two daughters. When she is not writing or reading, you will find her surfing and watch the dolphins play in the waves of the Atlantic Ocean.

Join Willow Rose's VIP Newsletter to get exclusive updates about New Releases, Giveaways, and FREE ebooks.

Just scan this QR code with your phone and click on the link:

SCAN ME

Win a waterproof Kindle e-reader or a $125 Amazon giftcard!

Just become a member of my Facebook group **WILLOW ROSE - MYSTERY SERIES**.

Every time we pass 1000 new members, we'll randomly select a winner from all the entries.

To enter go here:
https://www.facebook.com/groups/1921072668197253

Tired of too many emails? Text the word: "willowrose" to 31996 to sign up to Willow's VIP text List to get a text alert with news about New Releases, Giveaways, Bargains and Free books from Willow.